T0113727

Praise for *The Christmas Angel Project*

"Carlson's latest holiday offering is sure to become a fan favorite! Full of hope, it embodies all that is beloved about the Christmas season."

—*RT Book Reviews*

"A short novel packed with the true meaning of Christmas."

—*Fiction Addiction Fix*

Praise for *The Christmas Joy Ride*

"No one captures the heartwarming fun of the Christmas season quite like Melody Carlson."

—*Fresh Fiction*

"Popular and seasoned author Carlson skillfully draws readers into the lives of her characters."

—*Library Journal*

"For those that like a tidy ending with all the threads neatly tied together, Melody Carlson's *The Christmas Joy Ride* is just the thing. A light, sweet, and uplifting holiday story."

—*Christian Library Journal*

Books by Melody Carlson

THE
CHRISTMAS BLESSING

MELODY CARLSON

Revell

a division of Baker Publishing Group
Grand Rapids, Michigan

© 2017 by Carlson Management, Inc.

Published by Revell
a division of Baker Publishing Group
PO Box 6287, Grand Rapids, MI 49516-6287
www.revellbooks.com

Printed in the United States of America

Library of Congress Cataloging-in-Publication Data
Names: Carlson, Melody, author.
Title: The Christmas blessing / Melody Carlson.
Description: Grand Rapids, MI : Revell, [2017]
Identifiers: LCCN 2017006871 | ISBN 9780800722708 (cloth)
Subjects: LCSH: Christmas stories. | GSAFD: Christian fiction.
Classification: LCC PS3553.A73257 C465 2017 | DDC 813/.54—dc23
LC record available at https://lccn.loc.gov/2017006871

ISBN 978-0-8007-3759-7 (print on demand)

1

November 21, 1944
San Diego, California

Amelia Richards blinked back tears of hopelessness as she pressed the lid of her over-packed suitcase closed. Pausing to shove an escaped baby sweater sleeve back into the well-worn case, she snapped the last brass fastener with a click of finality.

"There." She stood up straight, trying to appear confident as she set the heavy suitcase by the bedroom door. "That's it then, Claudine. I'm packed and ready."

Her roommate, still in her pale pink bathrobe, looked worried as she gently rocked Baby James back and forth in her arms in an attempt to soothe him after a particularly bad bout of colic. "Are you sure you really want to do this?"

"I'm not sure about anything," Amelia confessed. She was too tired to think clearly at the moment. The baby had kept her up most of the night, and based on the headache pounding behind her eyes, she was probably getting the head cold that had been circulating around the beauty parlor where she worked as a hairdresser.

"You don't *have* to go." Claudine handed Amelia the baby. "I know it's been rough going lately, but we can make it work . . . somehow."

"You've already been more than generous." Amelia continued to jostle the baby, trying to settle him down and hoping he might take a little nap before it was time to leave. "It's not fair to you, Claudine. As much as I appreciate your help, Jimmy and I can't be your charity case." Amelia looked down at her fussing baby and sighed. "It's not fair to him either." She forced a smile. "And I'm guessing you won't miss us when Jimmy cries for his three o'clock feeding—or for several hours like he did last night."

"But how will you manage?" Claudine frowned. "Juggling your baby and luggage and a long train ride—all by yourself?"

With one arm holding Jimmy close to her, Amelia used the other to get her large handbag, which would also double as a diaper bag on this trip. Slipping the purse's strap over her shoulder, she picked up the bulky suitcase that she'd inherited from her grandmother and experimentally strolled through the tiny apartment. "See, it's not so bad," she assured Claudine. "I can manage just fine." She continued walking around, feeling her baby relaxing with the motion. Poor Jimmy had been fretting for several hours now—almost as if he was reflecting his mommy's stress. "Besides, I've heard that babies like riding on trains. I think the sound of the wheels on the tracks soothes them."

Claudine still looked skeptical.

"I just hope he doesn't disturb any passengers tonight. I'd hate to get us thrown off the train in the middle of nowhere."

"That's silly." But Claudine's brow creased as if she could imagine this. "What time do you arrive in Rockford tomorrow?"

"Early morning," Amelia spoke quietly. Jimmy was settling down now. "A little after seven I think."

"And you'll call me after you find a place to stay?" Claudine lowered her voice as Amelia nodded down to Jimmy's fluttering eyelids. "So I can send the rest of your things?"

"Yes, of course," she whispered. The limp weight of her baby told her that Jimmy had finally nodded off. "Not that I have much. Just those two boxes. They're in the bedroom closet. Hopefully out of your way."

"Thanks." Claudine pointed at the wall clock. "Well, you don't need to be to the station for a couple hours. And I've got a send-off breakfast almost ready for you."

"You're a doll." Amelia bent down to tuck her slumbering infant onto one end of the sofa, wedging a cushion against his back to keep him from rolling off. Not that the seven-week-old baby was doing much rolling yet, but according to the baby-care booklet her pediatrician had given her at Jimmy's first appointment—a pamphlet she studied almost like her Bible—one couldn't be too safe.

"It's only Spam and eggs and hotcakes," Claudine said as Amelia joined her in the kitchenette.

"*Only* Spam and eggs and hotcakes?" Amelia grinned as she sat down at the little plastic-topped table. "Sounds like a royal feast to me!"

Claudine set a cup of steaming coffee in front of her. "I really wish you weren't going. I'm still mad at Alliette for backing out on her promise to you."

"Alliette didn't know that Jimmy would have such a set of lungs when she told me I could bring him to work with me. It went well at first, but you saw how it's been the last couple of weeks. I know it bothered clients to hear him wailing like that. Especially if you consider how many women come to the beauty parlor to relax for a bit. And the truth is I got so rattled on my last day there that I nearly burned Mrs. Barnaby's hair with her permanent wave."

"But what about hiring a babysitter?" Claudine set a tempting plate in front of Amelia.

"You know I can't afford that. I'm barely getting by as it is." Amelia grimaced to think about her finances. She'd made a stringent budget for the trip, but she still needed to buy baby formula and a few other things on her way to the train station. The expenses of motherhood never ended. And without any employment lined up in Montana, she would need to keep close tabs on her cash.

"I still don't understand why you're not getting a pension from the War Department." Claudine scowled as she sat down with her own plate. "It shouldn't take them this long to sort through their paperwork, Amelia. Hasn't it been at least six months since James died in the war? You really should file a complaint against—"

"I'll sort it out in Rockford," Amelia said curtly. And now, although Claudine never said grace over a meal, Amelia bowed her head and prayed her usual silent blessing—adding in a petition for God to give her strength for the upcoming trip. "Amen," she proclaimed, opening her eyes to see Claudine watching with her usual amusement.

"You're such a *good girl*." Claudine used a friendly, teasing tone. "I'd say you were brought up right." Her smile faded. "Except that I know that's not true."

Amelia pursed her lips. She'd confided a lot about her past to Claudine this past year. But she hadn't told her everything.

"Sorry." Claudine looked genuinely contrite. "I know you don't like talking about your parents."

"That's right." Amelia picked up her fork. "And as far as my childhood and how it relates to my faith, I already told you that I found God through my grandmother when I was a teenager. My parents had nothing to do with it."

"I know, but I still think you should go to your mom and stepdad. You should demand that they give you some financial help. I'm sure they can afford it. And after everything your stepdad put you through—personally I think the lowlife should be in prison—*he owes you*. You should make him pay!"

Amelia inhaled sharply as she gave Claudine a severe warning look.

"Okay, okay." Claudine held up her hands in surrender. "I'm done. No more grousing about that. Like you've told me a dozen times, the past is the past."

"Thank you." Amelia's voice was husky and, once again, she worked to hold back her tears. If she wanted to make it through the upcoming days, she would need to contain her emotions. For some reason that had been no easy task of late. One of her beauty parlor customers had assured her that emotional ups and downs were to be expected with new mothers, but Amelia wasn't so sure.

"I know you're always saying you were born under an unlucky star, Amelia, but I keep thinking that one of these days your luck has to turn around." Claudine sighed. "Maybe this trip will do that for you—maybe your luck will change in Montana. Anyway, I hope it does."

"So do I." Amelia nodded as she forked her eggs.

"Now . . . I hate to keep nagging you about this, but did you ever write to James's parents? To let them know you're coming? Will they meet you and the baby at the train?"

Amelia slowly chewed, staring down at her coffee instead of answering.

"You didn't contact them, did you?"

Amelia took an uneasy sip of coffee.

"Even if you didn't do it yet, you can still send them a telegram from the train station. It will get there before you do. And remember you'll be arriving just one day before Thanksgiving. They might be busy. They should be expecting you."

"Don't worry. I'll deal with it," Amelia reassured her.

"It's like I keep telling you—ever since you heard the news about James—his parents will probably be thrilled to discover they're grandparents. I can't imagine why you'd want to keep it from them. I do understand your reluctance with your own parents, Amelia. They're not worth your time. But James's parents might be—"

"I'm going to tell you the truth." Amelia set down her fork, twisting the band of gold on her left hand nervously.

Claudine's eyebrows arched. "What?"

Amelia took in a deep breath, holding it as long as she could before the words exploded from her lips. "I lied to you." She watched Claudine's expression go from curiosity to confusion. It might not be easy, but Amelia knew this confession would be good practice for her. It wouldn't be long until she'd have to do it all over again—to James's parents in Rockford. Compared to them, telling Claudine was nothing.

"What do you mean?" Claudine sounded slightly angry now. "What did you lie to me about?"

"About James. He and I . . . we never got married."

Claudine's hand covered her mouth, and thankfully she said nothing.

"We met exactly like I told you—at the USO New Year's Eve dance." Amelia allowed her memory to meander back to that magical time in January. "James was so handsome in his Navy officer's uniform. As you know, he was a pilot, and had been serving in the South Pacific. Ever since the war began. He was in San Diego for some well-deserved leave time. He was supposed to have two whole weeks."

"Uh-huh?" Claudine's brow creased as she listened.

"Anyway, I was used to the attentions of servicemen. I'd been serving as a USO hostess for more than a year by then. Guys were always flirting with me . . . and I was adept at maintaining a safe distance. One guy even called me the Ice Queen. Not exactly flattering, but I tried to keep things cool. I always avoided any romantic involvement."

"Well, everyone knows that's against the USO rules," Claudine said. "But from what I hear, it happens all the time."

"Right . . . and that's what happened with James. I honestly couldn't help myself, Claudine. I fell instantly and hopelessly in love. I just knew he was the one for me and I suspected he felt the same. New Year's Eve was on a Friday, and we danced until the club shut down. Then he called on me the next morning—just hours later. We spent the whole day together . . . falling deeply in love. Sunday was even more magical." Amelia felt a lump in her throat. "On Monday, James came to the beauty salon and asked to take me to lunch. And that's when he got down on one knee to propose, complete with a beautiful engagement ring. Of course, I accepted."

"That's so romantic." Claudine sighed.

She nodded. "Yes, it was. James had even stopped by City Hall to get a marriage license application. We filled it out together and our plan was to get married the very next day. On Tuesday . . . January fourth." She paused to remember how wonderful that day had been. "We thought we'd have ten whole days to be together before James shipped out. But our plans were interrupted by the Navy that same afternoon. James was commanded to report back to his ship by midnight on Monday. His leave had been cut short because his aircraft carrier was shipping out."

"Why so soon?"

"James couldn't say, but I later began to suspect it was related to MacArthur's decision to move troops into the South Seas. The liberation has been in the headlines all year long—our Pacific forces driving out the Japanese. Naturally, they needed lots of pilots to launch air attacks and drop bombs."

"And that's probably how his plane got shot down."

Amelia nodded grimly. "I know this is no excuse, Claudine, but I think James knew that his chances of surviving the war were slim. He said as much to me on our last night together . . . I'm sure that's why I gave in to him. And, of course, I loved him."

"I know you did."

"I'm sure there are people who would judge me harshly for saying this, Claudine, but I don't regret what I did that night. Not really. If I had to lose James . . . well, at least I have Jimmy." She choked back a sob.

"Well, you don't have to tell people the truth, Amelia. Just let them all think you're a war widow. I'm sure there are lots of other women doing the same thing."

Amelia cringed inwardly. Living a lie wasn't easy. Not for her anyway. But she could keep her secret for the sake of her child. "I didn't find out until months later that James had been shot down in early February—he was killed just one month after we'd gotten engaged." Amelia used her napkin to blot her tears. "Plus I didn't even realize I was pregnant until March. It's embarrassing to say, but my mother had never told me the . . . you know, the facts of life. I was thirteen when I went to live with Grandma—to get away from my stepdad. But my grandma never talked about such things. Then she passed away shortly after I started beauty school."

"You've been through a lot in your life."

She nodded. "I suppose I was pretty naïve about men. I think I wanted to be oblivious."

Claudine pointed to the plain gold band on Amelia's ring finger. "You mentioned a beautiful engagement ring?"

"Right. Well, I finally went to the doctor—because I thought I had a stomach bug that I couldn't shake. Plus I was very blue about not hearing from James. I nearly fainted when the doctor told me the news. Then, after I recovered from the shock, I decided to pretend that James and I were married. I knew that was what James would want me to do. But to do that I needed a fresh start. So I quit my job and moved. And to pay my bills, I had to sell my engagement ring, but I got this one to make it look like I was married." She twisted the plain band. "When I got hired at Alliette's, I still didn't know that James had been killed. And I told myself that as soon as he got my letter informing him I was 'in the family way,' he would be allowed to return home, just long enough to marry me. I'd heard they do that for servicemen."

Claudine reached across the table, grasping Amelia's hand. "Oh, honey . . . I'm so sorry. That must've been terribly hard for you. But you could've told me the truth. I wouldn't hold it against you. I know these things happen."

"Thanks for understanding." Amelia sighed, remembering how kind Claudine had been to her on the very first day she'd gone to work in the beauty parlor. "When I got hired at Alliette's, it was important that you all believed I was a serviceman's wife. And I honestly thought I would be . . . as soon as James came home. In the meantime, I wanted to keep up a strong front."

Claudine squeezed her hand. "You've been a very brave woman."

"When I received only that one letter from James—sent shortly after he'd shipped out in January—I got worried. I wrote him again and again—and never heard a word back. Not even when I wrote him about my pregnancy. Then when my unopened letters were all returned to my post office box last May, well, I didn't know what to think. Either something very bad had happened to him . . . or else he'd changed his mind about marrying me. I honestly hoped that it was the latter . . . that way he'd at least be alive." She took another sip of coffee, hoping it would steady her nerves. "Then, last summer, after hearing so many news reports about war casualties in the South Pacific, I contacted the War Department."

"And that's when you learned he'd been killed?"

Amelia just nodded.

"So . . . do James's parents know about you?"

"I doubt that James had a chance to write to them. He barely had time to write to me. And it won't be easy telling them."

"Oh, my. You *are* a brave woman, Amelia."

Amelia wished that were true. She would need an extra-large portion of courage for this trip, and even more to face James's parents. But she thought she could do it—for little Jimmy's sake she'd have to face them. It looked like her only option. And it was the right thing to do.

2

Despite Amelia's claims that she could get herself and Jimmy to the train station via taxi, Claudine insisted on driving them. Because she lived within walking distance of Alliette's Beauty Parlor, it wasn't often that Claudine had an excuse to drive her rickety old Ford coupe. Claudine also insisted on caring for Jimmy while Amelia went into the drugstore to get formula and a few other things for her trip.

As Claudine was dropping them off in front of the train station, the reality of the situation kicked Amelia in the stomach. "Well, this is it," Amelia said in a shaky voice, blinking back tears as she put the strap of her oversized bag over one shoulder. Was she ready to leave her one true friend behind?

Claudine set Amelia's suitcase down on the sidewalk, then opened her arms to hug her. "You'll be just fine." She reached over to brush a loose strand of blonde hair away from Amelia's face, tucking it into the little black velvet hat. "You're the kind of girl who lands on her feet, Amelia."

Amelia sighed as she leaned down to scoop up Jimmy

from the car, holding him close. "I don't know what makes you think that."

Claudine patted Amelia's cheek. "I could say it's because you're so beautiful. And I still think you look like Donna Reed. So sweet and wholesome. If not for those blue eyes and your lighter hair color, you could be mistaken for her twin. But it's about more than just your looks, little darling. You've got spunk and resilience and gumption." She slowly shook her head. "Even more than I knew . . . after hearing the truth about you and James. I'll venture to say you're going to do just fine in Montana. And if you don't like it there, you come back here. I'll take you and Jimmy back." Claudine landed a kiss on top of Jimmy's blond head.

"I'm going to miss you terribly." Amelia felt the lump growing in her throat but was determined to be strong. "Thanks so much for everything." She leaned down to pick up her suitcase, but first looped the bulky winter coat over her arm. It felt like a balancing act. She just hoped she could get this load onto the train without an incident.

Claudine leaned over to kiss Amelia's cheek. "Something else you have, that I've observed—you have faith, Amelia. You've challenged my own." She slipped something into Amelia's coat pocket. "Something for later." She blinked almost as if she was tearing up too. "Now don't take any wooden nickels, darling—and you two take care!"

Amelia thanked her again. Then, feeling like a pack mule, she began to make her way through the station and toward the platform. Her load was more challenging than she'd expected, but it wasn't too long before she was safely aboard the train. To her relief, a helpful porter quickly prepared her sleeping car.

"I'm sure you and the little one will want to get settled in," he said kindly. "You let me know if you need anything. Food for you or bottles warmed for him. I am pleased to help you, ma'am."

Unsure if she should tip him, Amelia made her brightest smile as she thanked him, which—to her relief—appeared sufficient. He politely tipped his head as he quietly closed the door. He'd probably suspected, based on her shabby suitcase, that she was poor. She hung up the secondhand coat that Claudine had insisted she would need in Montana. It was in fairly good shape but smelled faintly of cigarette smoke.

Although Amelia would be on the train only until tomorrow morning, she unpacked a few things with the goal of making Jimmy and herself as comfortable as possible. To her delight, this cozy sleeping car felt just right for the two of them. Not only that, but as the train began to move, Jimmy relaxed and settled in. Almost as if he were glad they were finally on their way. Maybe he instinctively knew that life was about to get better for them. Perhaps he would enjoy meeting his paternal grandparents. At the moment the train pulled out of the station, anything seemed possible.

The train ride passed by blissfully and uneventfully throughout the day. Other than her sniffles, signaling that she probably was coming down with a cold, the trip so far was blessedly peaceful. The scenery, going from desert to mountains to timber country, improved by the hour. Amelia, who'd never been outside of Southern California, delighted in the beautiful sights she was witnessing along the way. The porter, true to his promise, was so attentive and helpful that she never had to leave her sleeping car for anything. He brought her lunch and dinner and checked frequently to see if Jimmy needed a bottle warmed.

In fact, it was all so perfectly serene that she honestly wished this trip might never end. From what she could tell, Jimmy—relaxed and content—probably wouldn't mind being a permanent resident on this train. But by bedtime her head was starting to throb from her cold and, knowing the porter would be knocking on her door at six in the morning, Amelia decided to go to bed early. Hopefully her cold would be on its way out by tomorrow.

It took Amelia a few seconds to get her bearings after waking to the sound of knocking on her door. But calling out a thank-you to the porter, she tumbled out of bed. She'd barely slept all night. Partly because of her fear of rolling over on Jimmy and partly because her mind had been spinning as quickly as the train wheels. What would happen when she got to Rockford? How would she get by?

As she fumbled about the snug sleeping car trying to get herself and the baby ready to disembark from the train, the small space suddenly felt confining and awkward. It was a good thing they were nearly done with their trip. Trying to find what she needed in her jumbled suitcase was a challenge. Not to mention her attempt to bathe poor Jimmy in the tiny sink. By the time she got him cleaned and dressed in one of the little outfits she'd sewn for him before he was born, she was exhausted.

Wedging him in a corner of the narrow unmade bed and ignoring his fussing, she got herself dressed and attempted to repack her bag. She was just sitting on the lid, getting it to close, when the porter knocked again.

"Can I take your bag, ma'am?"

She snapped the fasteners shut and opened the door. Thanking the porter for his help, she grabbed her handbag and picked up Jimmy, who was starting to cry even louder, and made her way out. "I'll take the baby to the coach car and try to quiet him," she whispered to the porter, "in case anyone is still trying to sleep."

He nodded with a grateful expression as he took her bag.

To her dismay, Jimmy's cries got louder as she sat down in the coach car, which thankfully was nearly empty at this early hour. She knew he was hungry but had hoped he could wait until they disembarked. Still, noticing the man glaring at her from across the aisle, she realized it would be selfish to force this stranger to endure her baby's wails. Judging by the man's rumpled brown suit, he'd probably been sitting up all night—probably more tired than she and no doubt in a foul mood.

Amelia opened her handbag, extracting the bottle she'd prepared earlier but hadn't had time to warm. Hopefully it would help calm her baby. But poor Jimmy took one eager sip and threw back his head, screaming louder than ever over the chilly temperature of his formula. She stood and, walking up and down the aisle, avoided the scowling face of the man in the brown suit as she tried to hush Jimmy's aggravated cries.

"Want me to warm that for you?" the porter offered as he hurried toward her.

"Yes, please." She eagerly handed him the bottle, then continued to walk up and down the aisle, trying to calm her son. To her relief, the man in the rumpled suit had left by now, and the porter soon returned with the warmed bottle. Thankfully, this did the trick for Jimmy and she was able to sit back down, taking a deep breath as she looked out the window to see golden rays of morning sunlight filtering through the majestic evergreen trees. She couldn't remember when she'd seen anything so lovely. All in all, this felt like the beginning of what was going to be a very good day.

Jimmy was just finishing his bottle as a quaint western town came into sight. It had to be Rockford—and it looked perfectly enchanting. Of course, it couldn't be more different than the warm beach town of San Diego, but it looked just like James had described it to her. "Like something out of a Western movie—like you expect to see John Wayne or Gary Cooper sauntering down Main Street," he'd told her with a grin.

Thoughts of James—or perhaps it was her head cold—made her eyes mist up. She used a clean diaper to dab away the tears, then settled it and Jimmy onto her shoulder, gently patting his back to bring up any air bubbles. With each pat, she tried to count her blessings. After all, they were almost there.

Jimmy would be meeting his grandparents soon. Maybe not for a few days—not until she had a chance to get the lay of the land. But she felt that James would have been proud of her for making it this far. At least she hoped he would have.

As the train slowed down, the porter returned to help her and Jimmy disembark. "I have something for you," she said before standing up. It was an extravagance for her meager budget, but she was so grateful for his generous assistance that she'd tucked a five-dollar bill into the side of her wallet. A sacrifice, yes, but this porter's help had been worth it. She reached into her purse, feeling around for her wallet, but it was missing.

"Oh no!" She laid Jimmy down in her lap as she used both hands to dig through her oversized purse, trying to find the misplaced wallet. "I must've lost it!" She quickly described the wallet to the porter as the train came to a stop. They looked all around and beneath her seat.

"Let's get you off the train and I'll go look in your sleeping car," he said as he led her to the door, helping her down the steps. "I'll tell the engineer to hold the train until I find it. You and junior wait right here."

Following his instructions, Amelia stood on the platform, where a cold, bitter wind was whipping through. She stared up at the sleek silver train, hoping that the porter would soon emerge with her wallet. Surely the kind, helpful man would soon find it—and then she would gladly tip him.

"I'm sorry, ma'am," he said as he bounded down the steps. "I looked everywhere for it. In your sleeping car. Down the aisles. Back in the coach car."

Amelia felt her heart pounding in fear. "But I can't go without—" The train whistle blew, snuffing out her words. "I'm sorry, ma'am." He jumped back on the train. "We gotta go. Have a schedule to keep."

She solemnly nodded, her eyes filling with tears as she watched him waving sadly. As the train slowly rumbled away, Amelia noticed a grim face peering out the window of a car toward the rear. The man in the rumpled brown suit—and he looked guilty! Had he stolen her wallet? She hated to think anyone could be so heartless, but he'd been right there while she was distracted with Jimmy, trying to hush him. She started to walk in the direction of the train, as if she could somehow stop it, but then realized it was pointless.

Standing on the end of the platform and watching the train getting smaller, Amelia felt the wind chilling the hot tears that spilled down her cheeks. It was icy cold out here! She pulled the knitted blanket more snugly around Jimmy, hurrying to gather her suitcase and get them both into the warm train station. The image of that selfish thief kept burning in her mind's eye. He had left her penniless. Everything she'd been able to save during the past several weeks, plus what she'd stashed away after selling her engagement ring and the few things left to her by her grandmother. It was all gone. Just like that. Her start-up funds for getting them settled in Rockford were gone. She and little Jimmy had nothing.

3

Amelia felt sickened—and not just from her head cold—as she carried her baby and suitcase into the train station. Going to a bench against the wall, she sat down and attempted to think. What was she going to do? Her original plan had been to find an inexpensive hotel room—a spot where she and Jimmy could acclimate themselves to Rockford for a few days. She could get her bearings, possibly do some investigative sleuthing into the mysterious Bradleys, and maybe even find gainful employment.

Due to her changed circumstances, she wondered if she'd need to revise her plan. Did this mean she should go directly to the Bradleys? How awkward would it be for them to have an unexpected guest showing up on the eve of Thanksgiving? Why hadn't she timed this differently? And yet James's parents might be glad to meet her. It was possible. She suspected they were good people—after all they had raised James—but the problem was she just didn't know this for sure.

Based on her experiences with her own mother and stepfather, she knew that people could look perfectly fine on the exterior, but be perfect monsters underneath. Amelia had no intention of exposing her baby to anyone who might possibly hurt him. And the truth was she knew next to nothing about Jimmy's paternal grandparents. She looked down on her now sleeping baby and, wrapping the thick knitted baby blanket more snugly around him, she gently laid him down on the bench beside her, using her handbag as a barrier to keep him from rolling. Just in case.

What to do? What to do? Amelia felt more helpless and hopeless than ever before. This dilemma wasn't only about her livelihood. She glanced down at her sweetly slumbering son and cringed. She was responsible for his sweet, innocent life as well. To find herself in such desperate straits was one thing—but to drag along a helpless infant . . . well, that was something else entirely.

Not for the first time Amelia wondered . . . Was she just incredibly unfortunate? Or was she—what her mother used to say—"dumber than dirt"? Maybe she was both. And perhaps Amelia deserved this nasty dark cloud that followed her everywhere. But Jimmy didn't!

Amelia knew she had a choice. She could either give in to despair and allow the black cloud to smother all traces of hope . . . or she could pray. Choosing to do the latter, she placed a steadying hand on Jimmy. Then, closing her eyes, she silently prayed, pleading with God to help them. There was no denying it was a frayed prayer of desperation—but stitched together by delicate threads of faith.

Amelia said a quiet "amen," then opened her eyes to glance around the train station. It appeared busier than when she'd first come inside. Perhaps this was due to the upcoming holiday. Tomorrow was Thanksgiving, and people were getting ready to head off on a journey or welcome someone just arriving. But no one was there for her. To her relief, none of them showed interest in the weeping woman and her baby occupying the bench against the wall.

She vaguely wondered if any of these people might be acquainted with James's family. According to James, when she'd quizzed him about his hometown during one of their few dates, Rockford was a pretty small town—a fraction of the size of San Diego. "But not so small that everyone knows everything about everybody," he'd assured her.

James hadn't shared very much about growing up in Rockford, or about his family. Just the bare-bones basics. He had two parents as well as an older sister named Grace who was married to a serviceman, and they had a little girl. But even knowing Grace's name wouldn't be much help since she'd be known by her married name.

And what if James's parents weren't the only Bradleys in town? Amelia certainly didn't plan to go knocking on doors, questioning strangers, or making a general nuisance of herself. In fact, she had no intention of showing up on James's parents' doorstep unannounced at all. She suddenly envisioned a desperate image of herself—the poor tattered woman with babe in arms as the harsh winter wind ripped mercilessly. Such a pitiful image might've been humorous. Except she was in no mood for humor.

She'd probably seen that melodramatic scene in some old silent movie as a child. Fine, maybe she was similar to that pathetic character—but she did not plan to present herself like *that*! It wouldn't be fair to her or her baby . . . and certainly not fair to James. She wondered if he'd ever written to his parents about her. But even if he had, he wouldn't have known about the baby.

With her face still damp from recently shed tears and her nose dripping from her cold, Amelia fumbled in her coat pocket in search of the fresh handkerchief she felt certain she'd tucked in there yesterday. As she extracted it, a white envelope tumbled out as well. It was slightly dog-eared and bent, and she wasn't sure where it had originated. Perhaps it was from the previous owner of the secondhand coat—a garment she was most grateful for now. Just then she remembered Claudine . . . Her friend had slipped something into Amelia's pocket yesterday, saying it was "for later."

Amelia dabbed her tears, then opened the envelope, expecting to find a sweet little note of encouragement. Instead, she pulled out five crisp five-dollar bills. Clutching this unexpected treasure to her chest, she thanked God for Claudine's kind generosity. Though not nearly as much as she'd lost in her stolen wallet, it was still enough to tide her and Jimmy over for a few days. Perhaps long enough for her to figure things out or even find work. *But where to begin?* She knew a cheap hotel would probably run around three dollars a night. And a taxi might eat up the equivalent of one night's lodging.

Still clutching her precious cache in her fist, she decided to walk to town. She had no idea how far it was to the nearest hotel, but right now she needed to pinch every penny. She tucked her money into a pocket inside her handbag, then secured the strap over her shoulder. Relieved that Jimmy was still sleeping, she wrapped the blanket more tightly around him and gently pulled his little blue knit cap down over his ears, then gathered him into her arms. Feeling, once again, somewhat like a pack mule, she grasped her heavy suitcase and slowly but steadily made her way to the front of the station, going outside to stand on the sidewalk and determine which way to go. Seeing taller buildings to her right, she started to walk.

Wishing she'd thought to button up her coat against the cold, she clutched Jimmy closer to her chest, walking as quickly as she was able toward the city center. Unfortunately it was also directly into the bitingly cold wind. It sliced through her like a knife. After a few minutes, Amelia began longing for the sunny warmth of San Diego. Oh, why had she ever thought going to Montana this close to winter was a good idea?

As she walked, her mind returned to that pathetic image from the stupid old movie—all Amelia needed to complete that picture was a small blizzard, and she wouldn't be surprised if that was coming. She'd never experienced actual snow before. Oh, she'd seen it in movies and on Christmas cards, and had always imagined it would be lovely, but this piercing Montana weather melted all interest in snow.

"Yoo-hoo? Hello there?" A middle-aged woman stuck her head out of a car window, waving vigorously. "Do you need a lift, honey?"

Amelia blinked in surprise then eagerly nodded. "Y-yes! That would be wonderful! Thank you!"

The old black car pulled next to the sidewalk and the

woman hopped out. "It's so cold today. I was just telling Fred, that's my husband there." She pointed to the man coming around from the driver's side now. "You and your poor baby must be half frozen."

"Here, let me take that." Fred reached for Amelia's suitcase. "I'll put it in the trunk."

"And you get in the backseat." The woman opened the door.

Suddenly Amelia was uncertain. She studied the woman's face for a moment, trying to discern her motives. Was Amelia a fool to get inside a car with strangers? What if it was irresponsible? Maybe these people wanted to kidnap her baby! She remembered the Lindbergh story. The plain-faced woman didn't really look evil. But looks could be deceiving.

"It's all right," the woman reassured her. "The kids are back there, but I asked them to skooch over to make room for you. Go ahead, get in before we all freeze to death."

Amelia peeked inside the car to see a boy and girl, squeezed together into half of the backseat. They looked to be grade-school age or maybe older, both curiously staring up at her. "Hello?" she said tentatively as she got inside. "I'm Amelia and this is Jimmy."

"I'm Susan." The girl poked her brother. "This is Rollin. He don't talk much."

"And I'm Clara," the woman said as the car began to move. "We just drove over from Idaho. Headed for my folks' place to celebrate Thanksgiving. We came a day early—so I could help my mom with the cooking since she broke her arm last week."

"Where are you going?" Fred peered back at Amelia as he stopped for the traffic light.

"I, uh, I'm not sure," Amelia confessed.

"Not sure?" Fred frowned.

"Well, I need to find a hotel." Amelia said quickly. "Or a place that rents rooms. But I can't afford anything too expensive. Someone stole my wallet on the train. That's why I'm walking."

"Stole your wallet?" Clara looked alarmed.

"Did you tell the police?" Fred asked.

"No." Amelia considered this. Maybe she should've. "I think the thief is still on the train. I don't see how the police could catch him now."

"Well, that's a low-down shame. Do you have family in town?" Clara asked. "To help you out?"

"Yes, of course," Amelia said quickly. And, really, it wasn't untrue. At least Jimmy had family. "But I don't want to stay with them. Do you know of an inexpensive hotel?"

"That'd be Wallace's," Fred told her. "It's nothing fancy, but from what I hear, it's clean. And it's only a few blocks from the station."

"I probably could've walked," Amelia murmured. Although she was grateful for the warm car.

"Not with that baby," Clara said. "And we don't mind, do we, Fred? Our chance to do a good deed. Rollin's a Boy Scout." She pointed at her son. "Your good deed for today can be to carry this lady's bag into the hotel for her."

After they dropped Amelia in front of Wallace's Hotel, silent Rollin got her suitcase and lugged it into the hotel lobby for her. Before she could even thank him, he darted back out. As she waited for the reception clerk, she got worried. What if this hotel was fully booked? What then?

To her relief, there was still a room available, but the cost of just three nights would use up nearly half of her limited funds. Still, what choice did she have? She needed time to figure things out with the Bradleys—and three days was cutting it very short.

"Can you recommend a babysitter for me?" Amelia asked the clerk.

"My daughter Dorothy babysits for guests sometimes," he told her. "When she's not in school. But not tomorrow, since it's Thanksgiving."

Amelia asked him a few questions about Dorothy and, satisfied the girl was old enough and experienced enough, she continued. "I would need her for a couple of hours this afternoon," she said. "Perhaps after she gets out of school?"

"No school today," he said.

"Oh, good. Then do you think Dorothy could come around one?"

"I don't see why not. Let's plan on it. Unless you hear otherwise from me, you can expect her."

She thanked him and, hoping her luck might be improving, rode the elevator to the third floor. Before long she was getting settled in her room. She removed a bureau drawer and lined it with a pillow from the bed to transform it into a temporary bassinet. Both she and Jimmy would probably sleep better tonight. In the meantime, she had much to do.

First she unpacked, putting everything away. Then she began to get everything ready for Dorothy the babysitter.

A part of her questioned the sensibility of having a stranger taking care of Jimmy. But really, what choice did she have? It wasn't as if she could drag the baby around with her. Especially not in this cold weather. Still, she reassured herself, she would check Dorothy out very carefully before leaving this afternoon. If she had any misgivings, she would simply tell the girl she'd changed her mind.

Amelia was just starting to long for a nap when she heard someone tapping on the door. Grateful that the teen girl knocked quietly, Amelia let her in, explaining that Jimmy was sleeping. "We had a long night on the train from California."

"You're from California?" Dorothy's brown eyes got big.

"Yes. San Diego." Amelia already liked this girl. She showed her around, pointing out where fresh diapers and a change of clothes were, as well as the clean baby bottles and formula. "But I should be back before his next feeding time," she whispered. "He just had a bottle half an hour ago. And I expect he'll mostly sleep. If he gets fussy just jostle him a bit and he'll probably quiet down." Amelia looked more closely at the neatly dressed girl. "You've had experience with infants, right?"

"Oh, sure. I babysat for my nieces and nephews when they were babies, and I was only twelve then. They're older now, but I still watch them sometimes."

"Good. Now do you have any questions?"

"I don't think so."

"I should be back by three."

"Okay. You can stay longer if you need to."

"Thanks." Amelia picked up her purse. "But two hours is probably fine." Amelia bent down to kiss Jimmy's cheek. "Be good," she whispered.

Amelia stopped by the reception desk before exiting the hotel. "Is there a good beauty salon nearby?"

The clerk grinned at her. "Not that you need it, but Beulah's Beauty Shop is just a couple blocks that way." He jerked his thumb to the left. "Pink-and-white awning, you can't miss it."

"Thanks. I wanted to inquire about employment there," she explained. "I'm a licensed beautician."

"Oh, yeah." He nodded. "Well, good luck with that."

"Thanks. And thanks for sending your daughter to me. She's a very nice girl."

His smile looked more sincere now. "Dot's a good girl. Very responsible."

"I appreciate that." She thanked him again and, feeling like Jimmy really was in good hands, exited the hotel. Thanks to the striped awning, which was snapping in the wind, Beulah's Beauty Shop was easy to find. But as soon as she stepped inside, she could see they were busy. With most of the beautician chairs occupied, there were still three women in the waiting area. Of course, it was the day before a holiday. Always a busy time for hair salons.

Feeling a bit guilty, but desperate, Amelia went to the reception desk and rang the bell. After a few minutes, a slightly frantic-looking redhead hurried over. "I'm sorry," she said quickly. "We're too busy to book any more appointments. Beulah's out today, and one of our girls is sick."

"I didn't want a hair appointment. I wanted to inquire about employment. I'm a licensed beautician. I just arrived from California and am looking for—"

"Sorry, as much as we could use help right now, the owner is gone so I can't really—"

"Why don't you let her do my hair?" A stout, gray-haired woman in the waiting area stood up and came over. "For Pete's sake, I've been waiting for over an hour for a cut and curl and I still have grocery shopping to do."

"Go ahead," the beautician nearest the reception area called out. "Let her take Mrs. Livingston. Beulah won't care."

The redhead still looked uncertain. "But we don't even know her."

"I'm Amelia." She stuck out her hand. "And I'd be happy to fill in if it'd help."

"Uh . . . okay." The redhead grasped her hand. "I'm Sally. Come with me and I'll get you a smock."

Amelia felt a rush of hope as she followed Sally into the back room. Imagine—finding a job on her first day in town! Too good to be true. Of course, she knew she didn't exactly have a real job yet. But this would be her chance to prove herself. Or, with her luck, she could end up being thrown out on her ear.

4

"I'll warn you," Sally whispered as she opened a closet in the back room, "no one likes working on Martha Livingston. She's a horrible gossip, and she likes to complain. The only reason I'm not worried about letting you take her appointment is that Beulah probably wouldn't care if we lost her business."

"Hopefully that won't happen."

Sally chuckled as she handed Amelia a pale pink smock. "Good luck just the same."

"Thanks." Amelia tied the smock's belt snugly around her waist as they went back out.

"You can use Peggy's station." Sally pointed to a vacant pink chair. "She's out sick today."

Amelia, remembering she was still trying to fight off her own bug, hoped she wouldn't share it with Mrs. Livingston. She quizzed the older woman about her hair expectations as she carefully tested the water temperature in the shampoo sink. Soon Amelia was gently but firmly massaging shampoo into the older woman's scalp. It felt right to be doing hair again, but the whole while Mrs. Livingston talked nonstop. Some was just idle chatter, but the woman was also very curious, asking where Amelia came from in California and what had brought her to Rockford.

Amelia attempted to keep her answers as vague as possible, but while towel drying Mrs. Livingston's hair she realized she might be missing out on an opportunity. "A friend of mine has relatives in Rockford," Amelia said in a nonchalant tone. "The Bradleys. I'm not sure what the parents' names are, but I believe they have a daughter named Grace and a—"

"You don't mean George and Helene Bradley?" Mrs. Livingston said suddenly.

"Well, I don't know if—"

"Their daughter's name is Grace. They had a son too. But poor James died in the war. Not that long ago. He'd been a pilot in the Navy for a couple of years. A bit of a wild hare as a kid, but he turned out to be a very nice young man. Such a loss." She made a tsk-tsk sound.

"Yes." Amelia concealed her eagerness to hear more. "That sounds like the family."

"So did you say you're friends with Grace?"

"No, not exactly. My friend, uh, is related to the family." In order to not feel deceitful, Amelia decided that her "friend" must be Jimmy. After all, he was related to the Bradleys—and what better friend did she have right now?

"So you're spending Thanksgiving with the Bradleys?"

"No, no. I don't even know them." Amelia needed to back-track. "I just mentioned them because of my friend's association . . . and I thought they lived here."

"Well, take it from me, Doc Bradley is the salt of the earth. You'd have to look far and wide to find a nicer man. But that wife of his, well, you can have her." She chuckled. "Not that you'd want her. But to be fair, I'm afraid Helene can't help her unfortunate disposition. It's the family she came from. You know what they say: the apple doesn't fall far from the tree."

"Really?" Amelia was starting to snip now, trying to stay focused on the haircut as she listened intently to each word.

"You see, Helene was a Jackson—they were one of the original founding families of Rockford. Made their money in copper mines. And when I was a girl, it seemed like the Jacksons owned most of the town."

"Some of them still do," the woman in the next chair said quietly.

Mrs. Livingston laughed. "That's for certain. I'm sorry if you're a friend of Helene's, but that woman sometimes acts like she's the queen of Rockford. No doubt she could buy and sell most everyone in town, but she doesn't need to lord it over the rest of us. Doc Bradley certainly doesn't."

"Maybe it's because his wife is the one with the money," someone else said.

"I'm sure Helene keeps poor Doc Bradley in his place too," Mrs. Livingston said.

"Oh, Martha, she's not that bad," Sally's client argued. "It's just that Helene is, well, as my Bernice would say, she's a *very straight stick*."

"She's a hard-nosed, stuck-up snob," Mrs. Livingston declared. "Did you hear what Helene Bradley did to young

Jeannie Campbell last week?" She turned her head so sharply it nearly resulted in losing a piece of ear. "Helene heard that Jeannie missed curfew last Saturday, and she used that as an excuse to dismiss Jeannie from volunteering for the American Red Cross. Can you imagine?"

"As chairwoman, that's Helene's right," the other woman said. "Though it is a bit harsh."

"Since when does staying out late mean you can't roll bandages?"

"Mrs. Bradley definitely has some high standards," Sally said. "But I'll give her this: she tips generously."

"Maybe so, but did you know she didn't speak to her very own daughter for two years?" Mrs. Livingston continued. "She was so mad that Grace married Harry Griffin I heard she wrote her daughter out of her will."

"Why was she so mad?" Amelia asked meekly.

"Helene didn't think Harry's family was good enough for Grace. The Griffins live in Missoula. They're firefighters. You know the fellows that jump out of airplanes to put out forest fires? Very exciting, I suppose, but Helene did not approve. Not at all. And she was fit to be tied when Harry got James interested in flying too." Mrs. Livingston locked eyes with Amelia in the mirror. "James was the son that got killed in the war. The reason he went in as a pilot was because he'd been working for Harry's family in Missoula. I heard he was a very good pilot. But I'm sure Helene feels that Harry is to blame for her son's death."

"That's ridiculous," the other woman protested. "It's the war that killed James, and Harry is fighting that same war.

Along with so many of our boys. If you want to blame anyone, blame the Axis. Blame stupid Hirohito and Hitler and Mussolini!"

"I know that well enough," Mrs. Livingston said irately. "But Helene Bradley might not see it quite like that."

"Was Mrs. Bradley on good terms with her son?" Amelia rolled the first curl around her finger, securing it with a pin. "I mean, before he died?"

"Hard to say. The truth is Helene Bradley isn't on good terms with much of anyone. No one measures up to her standards. And from what I hear, she's been more cantankerous than ever after losing her son."

"I think that's understandable," the other woman said. "I'd be out of sorts too if I lost a child. No parent wants to outlive their children. It's not right."

"That's true, but Helene was like that even before James died."

Hearing them speaking so openly about James made it harder than ever to maintain her composure, but now instead of listening to them going back and forth about the Bradleys, Amelia knew she needed to focus on getting Mrs. Livingston's hair properly set. To her relief, the old woman's thinning locks didn't take long to curl.

"We'll just put you under the dryer for a few minutes," Amelia told her as she wrapped the hairnet around the pin curls and led her to the dryer area.

While Mrs. Livingston's hair was drying, Amelia swept up the station, taking care to leave everything there in even better shape than she'd found it. Then, seeing that Mrs.

Livingston's hair was dry, Amelia brought her back to the station and carefully removed the pins. She brushed and styled it, applied some hairspray, and finally spun the old woman around to face the mirror. "How's that?"

Mrs. Livingston's brows arched as she reached up to touch her hair. For a long moment, Amelia couldn't guess her thoughts. Then she smiled. "Well, it's different than the way Peggy normally does it, but I think I like it better. Is this some new California style?"

Amelia wasn't sure how to answer, so she just nodded. "It looks lovely on you."

"Thank you." She patted the back of her hair with satisfaction. "I'll tell everyone that it's a California style."

"Now if you'll excuse me, I should probably go. I still have errands to run." Amelia could see that Sally and the other beauticians had things under control now, and feeling like her head cold was getting the best of her, Amelia went over to Sally. "Thanks for letting me step in like that," she quietly told her.

"Thank *you*!" Sally beamed at her. "I think Mrs. Livingston actually likes you—and believe me that's no small thing."

Amelia returned the smock to the back room, then came back to see Mrs. Livingston carefully pinning on her hat. "Do you happen to know where the Bradleys live?" Amelia asked quietly as she slipped on her coat.

"Oh, sure, everyone knows the Bradley mansion." She gave quick directions. "On Oak Street. That's just two blocks east of Main Street."

"Don't go before I pay you." Sally looked up from where

she was just starting to apply hair dye to a young woman's roots.

"You've got your hands full," Amelia told her. "How about if I stop back by here when it's not so busy?"

"That'd be great! Thanks!"

Amelia had severely mixed feelings as she exited the beauty parlor—and it wasn't just the shock of leaving the warm, bright salon to be hit with a gust of ice-cold wind either. As she buttoned her coat up to her chin and hurried down Main Street, she attempted to sort things out. On one hand, she was encouraged about the possibility of finding employment so quickly. But on the other hand, hearing about James's mother . . . well, it was unsettling to say the least. Helene Bradley sounded like a witch!

Even so, Amelia was determined to find the Bradley home. She had no plans to speak to anyone. She only wanted to see it for herself. The place where James had grown up . . . and where Jimmy's grandparents still lived. She was simply curious.

However, as she got closer to the neighborhood Mrs. Livingston had described to her, she could sense the affluence. The houses were bigger and grander and set farther apart, with long, tree-lined driveways and ornamental statues and ironwork. And, like Mrs. Livingston had said, the Bradley house was easily recognized. A three-story plantation-style white house with a large front porch and big round columns—it looked out of place in Montana. More like something from *Gone with the Wind*.

It wasn't just the overall grandness of the estate that impressed her, but the fact that everything about this place

looked like perfection. It was a very well-maintained property. It was clear to see that the Bradleys were a family of
influence in this town. But based on what Mrs. Livingston
had said, Amelia didn't think Mrs. Bradley's influence was
exactly positive.

Amelia hated to imagine Mrs. Bradley's reaction to the
news that James had gotten involved with someone like
Amelia. Besides the fact that her family was nothing to brag
about, Amelia knew that someone like Helene Bradley would
disapprove of having a grandbaby born out of wedlock.
She would probably be so ashamed of Amelia that she'd
disown Jimmy too.

Amelia walked quickly down the sidewalk that bordered
the front of the property. She tried not to stare, tried to act
like someone on a casual stroll. Although why anyone would
want to stroll in this freezing-cold wind was a mystery to
her. She paused by the hedge that grew alongside the wide
front yard, taking refuge from the wind and a moment to
carefully study the big white house. She wondered which
window might have been James's when he was growing up
there. Or perhaps his room had overlooked the backyard. She
also wondered why he hadn't told her that his parents were
so well off. Perhaps it was because she'd confessed to him
about her sad mess of a family. Maybe he hadn't wanted to
come across as boastful and proud. Or maybe it was because
he knew that his mother was a potential problem.

She was about to leave when a creamy yellow car came
down the street and turned into the driveway. Seeing the
face of a pretty young woman behind the wheel, Amelia

couldn't help but stare. Fortunately the woman appeared preoccupied with driving and didn't seem to notice she was being watched. The car pulled right in front of the house, and the woman, who wore dark green trousers and a plaid jacket, got out from the driver's side. A little girl wearing a fur-trimmed red coat leaped out from the other side. In the same instant the front door opened, a golden retriever dog came bounding out. The beautiful dog gave off some happy yelps as he ran back and forth, joyously greeting them. Then a tall, older woman with brown hair pinned in a sophisticated bun came out. She had on a plain charcoal-gray dress and was followed by a tall, white-haired man in a dark suit. They had to be James's parents—she just knew it! Dr. and Mrs. Bradley. So dignified looking . . . so respectable.

As the older couple went out to meet the young woman and girl—they had to be Grace and her daughter—it looked like the happy reunion of a perfectly normal family. Nothing like what Mrs. Livingston had described. Dr. Bradley swooped up the little girl in his arms, then hugged the young woman. Although Mrs. Bradley was more reserved, perhaps a bit on the cool side, she acted eager to welcome them.

As the four of them, followed by the energetic dog, went into the house, Amelia felt a wave of sadness wash over her. Like a child with her nose pressed to the toy-store window, she felt she was seeing something she could never have. She would never belong to these *fancy* people. They would never accept her. Besides the fact that they came from two completely different worlds, they would probably perceive Amelia as the wanton woman who'd borne an "illegitimate" child.

Someone who wanted to tarnish their deceased son's sterling reputation. And, really, who could blame them? It sounded horrible.

There was a chance they might not even believe her about her relationship with their son. What if they saw her as a gold digger, just out to get what she could from the bereaved family? Even if they did by some chance believe her, they would probably assume that she had been the bad influence in the relationship . . . that she was the one responsible for bringing James down to her level. Wasn't that how her own mother had treated her, back when her stepfather had taken advantage? Was Amelia prepared to face accusations like that?

Stifling the urge to cough, Amelia turned away and hurried back toward Main Street. She realized this damp air was probably not helping her cold. And she had a responsibility to take care of herself . . . in order to take care of her son.

As she walked, she replayed what Mrs. Livingston had said about the young woman who'd been kicked out of the Red Cross for missing her curfew. How much worse was Amelia's situation? How could she possibly expect the prim and proper Helene Bradley to welcome her and Jimmy with open arms? Amelia suspected that even if she presented the marriage license application that she and James had filled out on that Monday—in the hopes of standing before a judge the next day—Helene Bradley would still condemn her. But James had insisted on her keeping the application. He'd called it their guaranty that they would finish what they'd begun on his next leave of absence. Just the same, she didn't think it would make any difference for someone like Helene Bradley.

Of course there was James's father. She remembered how he'd swooped the little girl into his arms, the way he'd warmly embraced his daughter. Plus Mrs. Livingston had called him the *salt of the earth*. Maybe Amelia would have a chance with him. Although she knew better than to come between a married couple—it backfired to set one partner against the other. In the long run, they would both resent it . . . and then they would resent her, and probably her child as well.

On Main Street she found a store where she could do some very frugal shopping. Just the bare necessities, more formula for Jimmy and some nonperishable foods to get her through the next few days, plus a small, much-needed box of laundry soap. Her only "splurge" was a bucket that cost a quarter and would serve as a diaper pail. Tomorrow she would need to wash diapers as well as attempt to figure out her life . . . and her next steps. But as she carried her purchases home in her shiny new bucket, she couldn't help but feel she'd come to Montana on a fool's mission. Such a cold place to feel this lost and alone. What had she been thinking?

5

As Amelia laundered Jimmy's diapers—putting the pail she'd purchased the day before in the bathtub—she remembered that today was Thanksgiving. She didn't plan to do any celebrating. But as she wrung the water out of the clean diapers, she decided to mentally list the things she was thankful for: (1) Jimmy, and that he was peacefully sleeping after a restless night. (2) Laundry soap and the bucket, as well as the radiator she was using to dry Jimmy's clean diapers. (3) Enough formula to last Jimmy about four more days. (4) A can of Spam, an apple, and a hard roll that would serve as her "Thanksgiving feast."

As she hung the last diaper near the radiator, Amelia realized she was tired of the thankful game. The truth was she didn't feel thankful for much of anything. What kind of life was this? Stuck in a stuffy hotel room, washing diapers, eating a meager meal by herself? Not to mention her cough was getting worse and she was worried that Jimmy had caught her bug as well. She'd awakened several times to the sound of him making little coughing and wheezing sounds himself. What would she do if he got sick?

As she tidied up the bathroom, she considered asking Claudine for help. She'd already called her collect to inform her that she had safely arrived as well as to thank her for her generous gift. But she hadn't mentioned getting robbed on the train or how hopeless she felt about getting any help from James's parents. Claudine had sounded so bubbly and happy, telling Amelia about how Hank Snyder had called her "out of the blue" to invite himself to her apartment for Thanksgiving. And Amelia knew how Claudine had been pining for this guy to come back into her life. It was probably much easier to do when Claudine wasn't saddled with a roommate and baby.

No, Amelia decided as she proceeded to do some of her own laundry in the bathroom sink. She had to figure her way out of this on her own. She was a grown woman who'd gotten herself into this situation. It was up to her to manage it on her own.

By the time she was hanging her damp laundry on the bed frame, she was making a plan of sorts. First thing tomorrow morning, she would go back to Beulah's. To save money for babysitting, she'd take Jimmy along with her. But first she'd dress him up in the little blue suit she'd made him from a piece of fabric she'd saved from cutting down one of her long skirts. The shorter hemlines that had come with the war, a result of the government's effort to conserve cloth, had left a number of nice remnants that Amelia had stashed away—and these pieces had been just right for sewing baby clothes. Not for the first time, she was grateful for Grandma teaching her to sew. There, she thought, something else to add to her Thanksgiving thankful list.

Amelia would put on her best blue suit, which perfectly matched Jimmy's. Claudine had been so impressed that she'd insisted on taking a photo of Amelia and Jimmy in their "clever" matching outfits. Hopefully Claudine would get her film developed and send the photograph someday.

So, dressed in their blue suits, Amelia and Jimmy would go to Beulah's and attempt to make a good impression. Hopefully Sally would be there and she would remember her promise to pay Amelia for doing Mrs. Livingston's hair. If she was lucky, there would be a tip, although Amelia wasn't counting on it. Maybe the owner, Beulah, would be there and Amelia could ask her about employment. Perhaps she'd be impressed that Amelia had handled a difficult customer.

By the time Amelia was sitting down to her meager midday meal, she was feeling somewhat encouraged. Tomorrow was a new day and she would make the most of it. She would grab onto her future with both hands—and somehow she would make it work!

But as the day wore on, Amelia's optimism wore down. Not only was her cough getting worse, she suspected that Jimmy was running a fever now too. They were both sick. As hard as she tried to comfort him, feeding him whenever he cried, she knew that it wasn't enough. Plus her energy was rapidly fading. But the more she longed to simply collapse onto the bed and sleep, the more Jimmy needed her.

Not only that, but because there were other guests in the hotel, she knew she needed to do whatever it took to keep him pacified and quiet.

By midnight, Amelia was completely exhausted. To make matters worse, as she prepared another bottle of formula she realized how much she had used throughout the day. Even though Jimmy didn't finish a full bottle, she would make him a fresh one whenever his fussing grew intense—partly to quiet him and partly because she felt he needed more fluids. But now she knew she didn't have enough formula to last much more than a day.

In the wee hours of the morning, while rocking her fussing infant, Amelia mentally calculated what little money she had left, along with the cost of her lodging plus minimal expenses. She realized even if Sally paid her for Mrs. Livingston, Amelia wouldn't have enough to get by more than a couple of days.

Her dire straits would force her to complete her original plan—she had to go to James's parents for help. This meant swallowing what little pride she had left, confessing her uncomfortable truth, and begging for their mercy. It wasn't something she could do for herself, but she knew she could do it for Jimmy. Because it was his only hope.

6

On the day after Thanksgiving, Helene Bradley woke up sobbing. As she climbed out of bed, she noticed that her pillow was soaked with tears. Had she been crying in her sleep again? Well, at least George was already up. Probably out walking the dog since he had no appointments until Monday. Hopefully Janie had gone with them. It was sweet seeing how much their granddaughter loved their golden retriever. Last night Janie had insisted that Goldie sleep in her room.

As Helene blew her nose and splashed cold water on her face, she was relieved that George wasn't here to witness her misery. It was distressing for him to see her like this. It was disturbing to her too. Especially since Helene Bradley was known for being "cool as a cucumber"—and worse. She wasn't particularly fond of those labels, but she'd grown used to them over the years.

Still, it had been nearly ten months, and George had expected her to move forward by now. So much so that he'd even suggested tranquilizer pills. But she'd firmly declined. Promising to do better. As a result, she'd been striving to keep up appearances, and she'd gotten quite adept at her pretenses. But sometimes, like this morning when she'd woken from the dream where she couldn't make her way to her only son, she missed him so much that the ache deep inside of her felt unbearable. Oh, she knew she wasn't the only mother to lose a son to this horrible war. But how did other parents go on? How did one survive losing a child? How could she live in a world that didn't have James in it?

As she carefully dressed in her recent "uniform"—gray woolen skirt and a cashmere sweater set, she reminded herself that she still had Grace and Janie—and that they were here at the house. That was something to be grateful for. Really, it was hard to feel blue when Janie was about. But it was also hard to maintain her happy act in moments like this. Hopefully she would be better by breakfast time.

By the time Helene went downstairs, she could hear the sounds of cheerful voices below. It sounded as if everyone was up. Pasting a smile on her face, she went into the front room to see George and Janie playing checkers. Goldie was stretched out by the fireplace where an inviting fire was crackling. And Grace was curled up in an easy chair with a magazine. The perfect picture of familial contentment. No one would guess by looking at them that they had lost a loved one last spring.

The four of them had breakfast together, and the day continued in a hazy, lazy sort of way—playing board games with Janie, reading books, just being together in a warm and comfortable home. It wasn't until early afternoon that Helene was reminded of the missing family member.

MELODY CARLSON

"Are we going to put up the manger set today?" Janie asked hopefully.

"Oh . . . I don't know." Helene tossed an uneasy glance at her husband. It had always been their family tradition to set up the life-sized nativity scene on the day after Thanksgiving, but she'd hoped that no one would mention it today. The idea of seeing those painted plywood pieces . . . the holy family and shepherds and such . . . well, she just wasn't sure she could keep her emotions in check.

"Of course, we are," George said cheerfully to Janie. "Today is the day."

"See, I told you," Grace assured her daughter. "We always put the nativity set up on the day after Thanksgiving. It's tradition."

"And Uncle James made all the pieces?" Janie asked. "Mary and Joseph and the donkey and the cow and everything? He made all of them when he was just a little boy?"

"Well, he wasn't a *little* boy," Grace explained. "I think James was eleven or twelve when he first started it. And it took him a few years to complete all the figures. As I recall he made the three wise men in high school."

"And when he was younger, I had to help him cut out the pieces of wood," George explained. "But Uncle James took over later on. And he did all the painting himself."

"Was Uncle James an artist?"

"He could've been," Helene said sadly. "Such talent. But he wanted to fly airplanes instead."

"He wanted to serve his country," George said somberly. "Uncle James was a real war hero."

55

"Like Daddy?" Janie asked with wide eyes.

"Yes." Grace sounded uneasy. "A lot like Daddy."

"Will Daddy die too?" Janie's voice sounded small and worried.

Everyone got very quiet and Helene and George exchanged concerned glances.

"No, of course not," Grace assured her. "Daddy will come home to us."

"Excuse me." Helene slowly stood, trying to hold back the emotions washing over her. "I need to go over tonight's dinner menu with Lydia."

"And *then* will you help us put up the manger set, Grandma?" Janie looked hopefully at her.

"Of course, she will," George reassured Janie, winking at Helene. "After all, Grandma will want the last word to make sure it's set up properly—everything in its place."

"That's right." Helene forced a smile for her granddaughter's sake, then went into the kitchen where Lydia had just sat down to her own lunch.

"Do you need something?" Lydia started to stand. "Do you want tea or—?"

"No, no. We don't need a thing." Helene put a hand on the woman's shoulder. "Sorry to disturb you." She reached for her handkerchief, using it to blot a careless tear. "I, uh, I just needed to escape for a moment . . . didn't want Janie to see me like this." She let out a little sob as she filled a glass with water, taking a quick sip.

"Oh, you poor darling." Lydia sadly shook her head as she came over to put an arm around Helene's shoulders.

"You're missing your boy again. I hear it's always hardest during holidays."

"I'm sure that's true." Helene quickly explained about the nativity scene. "I just don't know if I can hold it all in . . . it will be so difficult . . . seeing the nativity pieces out . . . so many memories." She took another sip. "But I know that I must . . . for Janie's sake."

"And for James's sake too," Lydia said firmly, looking directly into Helene's eyes. "That dear boy will be peering down from heaven, Mrs. Bradley. I just know it. And he'll be so happy to see you're still putting his nativity up. You must do it to honor him."

Helene considered this. "Yes, Lydia, I think you're right." She glanced toward the back staircase. "I think I'll go up this way. Thank you, Lydia. Thank you very much."

As Helene made her way up the servants' staircase, she wished she was stronger and braver. She didn't know how George and Grace always managed to keep their emotions in such close check. Especially since she'd always been so adept at concealing feelings. So much so that some people in town thought her heartless. Perhaps it would be preferable to be heartless. Then she could avoid such intense pain. And regrets.

Amelia had no doubts that Jimmy was ill. His cough, like hers, had grown worse throughout the night. And despite her plans to take him with her to the beauty salon today—and to beg for a job—she knew that would be irresponsible. So she called Dorothy, asking her to babysit for a couple of hours in the afternoon. Yes, that would further deplete her diminishing finances. But it was necessary. Amelia knew what needed to be done—and she intended to do it.

She did her best to get ready, putting on her best suit and neatly styling her hair, but when she saw herself in the bathroom mirror, she knew she resembled death warmed over. So much so that she was tempted to put on a bit of rouge and lipstick. But not wanting Helene Bradley to perceive her as a painted lady, she refrained. As she walked to the Bradleys' home, Amelia rehearsed the words she planned to say. Imagining herself ringing the doorbell and it being answered by a servant—since that big house just had to have servants—she would politely ask to speak to Dr. and Mrs. Bradley. And if she were questioned about this, she would simply say it was a family matter . . . and *private*. That should get her into their home.

Then, hopefully, she would meet James's parents in a private room and she would slowly tell them the full story of her and James. She would tell it honestly, but in such a way as to win their trust . . . perhaps even their compassion. She would explain how they had intended to be married, how they'd even filled out their marriage license paperwork, but how he'd been unexpectedly called back to the ship. Somehow she would make them understand that—in their hearts they had been married. At least that's what she hoped to do.

Walking the few blocks to their house sapped all her energy . . . as well as much of her nerve. By the time the grand white colonial home came into view she was breathless and struggling not to cough uncontrollably. Even so she was de-termined to do this—for Jimmy.

As she reached the edge of their property she saw Dr. and Mrs. Bradley, along with their daughter and granddaughter and the beautiful golden dog, putting together what appeared to be a Christmas nativity scene in the front yard. She didn't know what to do.

She couldn't imagine walking up to these people, inter-rupting their activity and announcing who she was, her con-nection to James, and why she was here. Certainly not in front of the little girl and James's sister. She lurked behind a nearby hedge for a long minute, just watching them as she tried to revise her plan. But seeing the dog starting to trot her way, Amelia knew she needed to move on. This was just not going to work.

It felt like it took forever to go the few blocks back to Main Street. And although the hotel was just a couple more blocks, she was so exhausted that it felt like miles. Then, see-ing Beulah's Beauty Shop, Amelia remembered the money that Sally had promised. Thanks to her inability to approach the Bradleys, she would need it more than ever. But to her dismay, Sally wasn't working today.

"And Beulah won't be back until Monday," the beautician working there informed Amelia. "Do you want to leave a message?"

"No, thank you." Amelia covered her mouth as she coughed. "I—I'll come back later."

The beautician peered curiously at her. "Are you okay, honey? You don't look too good."

"I, uh, I've got a cold," Amelia said quickly. "Just need some rest." She backed away and, feeling like she had the plague, she tried not to cough as she exited the parlor. Feeling weak and defeated, she made her way back to her hotel room.

"You were only gone an hour." Dorothy frowned. "You promised me two."

"I'll pay you for two." Amelia dug out the correct change, dropping it into her hand. "Thank you for watching him." She started coughing again.

"Thank you. It's probably good that you're back, because Jimmy is sick," Dorothy told her. "You should take him to the doctor."

"Yes, I know. I plan to do that." Amelia nodded. "Today."

"Oh, good." Dorothy got her coat, hurrying out as if she was worried she might catch whatever it was they had. And maybe she would . . . and that would probably be Amelia's fault too. Did she ever do anything right? It sure didn't feel like it.

She went over to check on Jimmy, relieved to see that he was sleeping. But his cheeks were flushed and his breathing sounded raspy. Still, she didn't want to disturb him. If he would just sleep a bit longer, perhaps she could rest too. They both needed rest. Still fully dressed in her good blue suit, she lay down on the bed . . . falling almost instantly asleep.

When she awoke it was to the sound of Jimmy's muffled sobs. His cries were so much quieter than usual, but she suspected it was simply because, like her, he was worn out from being sick. She fixed him a bottle and sat down to feed him. Watching him lying limply in her arms, looking so frail and helpless—and sick, she suddenly knew what she needed to do. It was as plain as day.

With crystal clear clarity—almost as if she'd heard the voice of God—she knew that she had to take Jimmy to his grandparents. She needed to do it straightaway. It could not wait until tomorrow. *Jimmy's grandfather was a doctor!* He would know exactly what to do to get Jimmy well. It was the only thing that made sense. And suddenly she knew just how to do it. Oh, some might call it a coward's way out, but she felt certain it would work.

7

By late afternoon, Helene was weary of the manufactured smile she'd been wearing the last couple of days. But Grace and Janie wouldn't be here for long, and after they were gone, Helene knew she could return to her melancholy routine.

"Grandpa is going to put the lights on the nativity scene," Janie exclaimed with enthusiasm as she ran into the front room where Helene and Goldie were settled next to the crackling fire.

"Yes, it's about time for the lights." Helene glanced outside to see the sun had already dipped below the trees. "Not a moment too soon."

"And I got this!" Janie's enthusiastic tone brought Goldie to her feet, eagerly wagging her feathery tail as Janie came close enough for Helene to see what looked like a doll cradled in her arms. Goldie sniffed them both with interest.

Janie held up the bedraggled doll for Helene to see. "Mama found her old baby doll in the attic. Her name is Mary Jane." Janie giggled. "Just like me. But I didn't look like *this* when I was a baby—did I, Grandma?"

Helene studied the well-worn doll. It had to be at least twenty years old. The hair had long since been rubbed off and the tip of its nose looked as if something had gnawed on it. "No, no, you were much prettier as a baby, Janie. But your mama's doll used to be better looking too."

"I'm going to put it in the manger. Mommy said Uncle James never made a Baby Jesus out of wood because he could never get it to look just right."

"That's true."

Janie stared down at the doll. "Is it okay for our Baby Jesus to be a girl doll?"

"I think it's just fine." Helene felt Goldie rest her head in her lap. Stroking the dog's silky coat, Helen realized how much the elderly dog had been enjoying the lively company in their house these past couple of days. Poor Goldie would probably be depressed to see them go.

"Mama asked Velma to find an old sheet to wrap up our Baby Jesus. That will be his *swaddling clothes*." Janie laughed. "That's such a funny word. *Swaddling*. What does it mean, Grandma?"

Helene explained it was a way to wrap up a baby.

"I wanna put Baby Jesus in the manger before Grandpa turns on the lights. I mean, after we get the swaddling clothes on the baby." Janie sat down next to Goldie, fiddling with the buttons on the doll's faded pink nightgown.

As Helene gazed out the window to where the shadows were steadily lengthening, she longed for an excuse—any reason to avoid looking at the homemade nativity scene again. Perhaps she could feign a headache. It had been hard enough watching the life-sized wooden pieces being set up earlier . . . remembering how hard her only son had worked to cut and paint them. And then remembering how James would take charge, commandeering his family about until all the figures were perfectly arranged . . . *just so*. The lighting had to be perfectly set up too. Then just after sundown, they would all watch as the lights came on. *Tradition*. But when James was shot down by the Japanese, it felt as if tradition had died with him. Or should've.

"I've got the swaddling clothes," Grace announced. "Let's wrap up that baby and get him outside. Grandpa is out there waiting for us—ready to turn on the lights."

The three of them, with Goldie curiously looking on, managed to twist and wrap the white twin sheet around and around the doll until everyone was finally satisfied. Janie triumphantly held up the bundle. "I think Uncle James must like it too."

Grace sighed. "Yes, honey, I'm sure he does."

"Do you think Uncle James is watching us? From up in heaven?" Janie asked as they headed for the front door.

"I think he's been watching," Grace told her as she helped her into a coat.

The three of them, accompanied by an eager Goldie, ceremoniously carried the swaddled baby out into the front yard. George was already there making some final adjustments on the three spotlights. James had rigged up the lights himself, always insisting it took three lights to properly show off all the figures.

With Goldie chasing her, Janie made a beeline for the

wooden manger that she'd already filled with straw. Like a nervous little mother, she took a moment to rearrange the straw, making sure it was fluffed just right. Helene shivered in the cold, averting her eyes from James's nativity pieces. Maybe this would be less painful next year . . . maybe time would heal some of her wounds.

Helene wanted to urge Janie to hurry up but knew that would sound impatient. Best to just bite her tongue and bide her time. This would soon be over with and they would all go inside where it was warm. Sensing a movement on the sidewalk behind her, Helene glanced over her shoulder, but seeing nothing, she turned back around and shoved her hands into her pockets.

Amelia had been well aware of how cold it was outside. For that reason she had dressed Jimmy in several layers of clothing, finally putting him into the fuzzy baby bunting that Claudine had gotten for him before they'd left for Montana. Then she'd taken a moment to write a quick note that she'd tucked into a clean and neatly folded diaper.

She'd filled the baby bottles with the last of the formula. Padding the glass bottles with clean diapers and the rest of Jimmy's tiny clothes, she packed it all into a grocery sack that she tucked into her emptied handbag. With Jimmy bundled into a baby blanket and the handbag looped over her arm, she tried to act perfectly natural as she carried him through the reception area of the hotel.

"Just getting some fresh air," she cheerfully informed the

reception clerk. Thankfully it wasn't Dorothy's dad manning the desk right now. "A little walk to clear the head."

It was just starting to get dusky as she went outside. Despite her weariness, she walked quickly toward the Bradleys' neighborhood. Her plan was to sneak up to the house, lay her precious bundle and the grocery sack on their doorstep, ring the bell, and run as fast as she could for the cover of the hedge. She knew it would be a pathetic scene—similar to the one she'd imagined earlier from the old silent movie. But somehow it all made sense. If she could get Jimmy into their hands without disclosing the truth about her and James it would probably be better—at least for Jimmy.

She'd decided earlier today that no child should be shadowed by his parents' questionable history. No child should be labeled with words like "illegitimate" or worse. Yes, this was the only way to give Jimmy a fair chance. And if he was as sick as she believed, well, it might very well save his life. That was something she was unable to do by herself.

When she reached the Bradley property, she was startled to see that once again the family members were outside. It made no sense. Why were they walking around their yard when it was so cold out and nearly dark? She paused in the shadows of the nearby laurel hedge, peering through the leaves as she listened to the sounds of their cheerful voices. Once again, the golden dog was there too, merrily trotting about as if they were having some sort of lawn party. But in the cold and dark? That was crazy.

Then suddenly, almost like magic, bright lights went on and the nativity scene they'd been working to assemble earlier burst into golden illumination. The Bradleys all clapped and cheered. Amelia blinked to see the amazing scene in front of her—a truly lovely nativity with a life-sized and realistic-looking Mary and Joseph kneeling next to a manger. They were surrounded by shepherds and sheep, three wise men, and numerous barn animals. It was amazingly lifelike! So much so that, for a moment, Amelia forgot what she was doing or why she was there.

When Jimmy started to quietly fuss, she suddenly remembered. She jostled him from side to side and he quieted . . . while she continued to watch and to wait. The scene was incredibly beautiful, but hopefully the Bradleys would soon get cold and go back into the house. Then, just like that, Dr. Bradley gathered up the little girl, hoisting her up to his shoulders, and all of them, trailed by the dog, started for the house. About halfway there, the dog turned around, and Amelia could see it coming her way. Had the curious animal sniffed a stranger in the yard? Hopefully it wasn't about to bark and reveal her whereabouts.

"Good boy," she whispered as the dog came closer, clearly aware of her presence. "It's okay. We can be friends."

The Bradleys were nearly to the porch when the dog started to sniff her. Then it let out a curious bark. Not threatening, just interested. "It's okay," she said quietly as she made her way into the yard. "This baby belongs here. He needs Dr. Bradley."

Now someone was calling for the dog. Apparently the dog's name was Goldie. Feeling her plan unraveling, Amelia glanced at the nearby nativity and suddenly realized that held her answer. Running directly for the manger, she reached inside and, removing what looked like a baby doll, she gently nestled Jimmy into its place. With tears streaming down both cheeks, she bent down to kiss him. "God bless you," she whispered. "God bless you and keep you."

Afraid that the family would spot her, she turned to run. But halfway across the yard, she remembered the baby things in her purse. Pausing to drop them in the grass, she took off again, heading for the cover of the laurel hedge.

She could hear the dog barking louder now. Not viciously, but with canine excitement. To Amelia's relief, the dog—Goldie—had remained by the manger. It almost felt as if she'd stayed there to guard Jimmy—and to alert her owners. "God bless you, Goldie," Amelia whispered. "God bless my baby."

Amelia knew she couldn't remain there and not expect to be found. So, using every last ounce of her energy, she ran all the way back to the hotel. It wasn't until she was breathlessly going inside that she realized she was still cradling the doll in her arms. Fortunately, the desk clerk was preoccupied and barely looked up to say hello. Holding the lifeless doll tightly to her chest, she hurried into her room, collapsing on her bed and sobbing uncontrollably.

8

As they went onto the front porch, Helene called out for Goldie again. But instead of coming, the dog just let out a couple of barks. "What's wrong with that dog?" Helene said absently, unbuttoning the top of her coat.

"She probably saw a squirrel," Janie suggested.

"Or that stray cat that's been hanging around." George opened the door and flipped on the porch light.

Helene turned back to peer into the yard. The spotlights were still illuminating the nativity scene, so brightly that she had to squint to see around them. "Come on, Goldie!" she called out. "Come on, girl. Time to go inside." But still Goldie didn't come.

"What's that dog up to?" George eased Janie down off his shoulders, whistling for Goldie to come.

"I don't know." Helene frowned. And suddenly Goldie was barking in a way that would probably disturb the neighbors.

"Why is Goldie making such a fuss?" Grace asked.

Helene called her dog again, but instead of coming like she'd been trained to do, Goldie started barking even louder.

"Something's wrong." Helene started out across the yard again.

"Wait," George called, but Helene continued and soon they were all walking back toward the nativity together.

"Is that a *baby* crying?" Grace asked as they got closer.

"Maybe it's Baby Jesus," Janie said in a matter-of-fact voice.

"That's impossible." Helene walked even faster.

"It does sound like an infant," George said in a worried tone.

They all hurried to the wooden stable, where Goldie stood at attention in front of the little manger. She was still barking, but her tail wagged in a friendly way. There, to everyone's stunned surprise, lying in the straw, was a real live baby, crying loudly.

Helene felt slightly faint as she went closer. "Oh, my—"

"It *is* a baby!" Janie squealed in delight. "Is it Baby Jesus, Mama? Is it? Is it?"

"No, of course not." Grace turned to Helene with wide eyes. "Where did it come from, Mom?"

"I have no idea."

"Maybe God put it here," Janie said. "Like Baby Jesus."

"I'm going to look for whoever left it," George announced.

As her husband marched off toward the sidewalk and street, Helene stooped over and, without even thinking, picked up the wailing child. She rocked it back and forth in her arms, attempting to calm the poor thing.

"Hush up, Goldie," Janie told the dog who was still barking. "You're scaring the baby."

"Whose baby is it?" Grace quietly asked Helene. "How did it get here?"

"I don't know," Helene told her. "But let's get it inside and out of the cold." She was already heading back to the house.

"Come on, Janie and Goldie," Grace commanded. "Let's go in the house with Grandma."

"What about Grandpa?" Janie called out as they followed Helene.

"He'll be fine," Helene called over her shoulder as she went up the front porch steps. "Let's get inside. Quickly."

As they all poured into the well-lit foyer, Helene was able to get a good look at the crying baby. His chubby face was flushed and pale curls were stuck to his damp forehead. Grace and Janie pressed in, trying to see him too.

"He's wrapped in blue," Grace observed. "Maybe he's a boy."

"He *is* a boy," Janie declared. "I can tell."

As Helene rocked the baby, which appeared to be bundled up in plenty of clothes, she suspected they were right. It did appear to be dressed like a male child. "Hush, hush," she said as she continued into the front room where, to her relief, the child stopped howling. But it still looked clearly unhappy and uncomfortable. The infant's cheeks were flushed and its nose was running. Probably from being out in the cold.

"Poor thing." Helene used her handkerchief to wipe his drippy nose. "Who do you belong to, little boy blue?"

"Can we keep him?" Janie asked as she looked on with curiosity.

"Of course not," Grace told her. "This baby belongs to someone else."

Helene sat down in an easy chair near the fireplace and, still trying to soothe the agitated child, she attempted to sort through the questions racing through her head. Where had he come from? Who did he belong to? Had he been abandoned? And if so, why in their manger?

"What are we going to do with him?" Janie looked at Helene with wide eyes.

"I guess we'll have to take care of him until his parents are found."

"Do you think someone kidnapped him?" Grace asked in a slightly horrified tone.

"I honestly don't know." Helene peeled off the baby-blue blanket wrapped around him and then began to remove the blue bunting. "It looks like someone really bundled him up though."

"They wanted him to stay warm," Janie suggested.

"Well, he'll be too warm in the house." Helene continued to remove layer after layer of clothing. "Goodness," she said when she got down to just one layer of clothing. He's not as big as I thought. I wonder how old he is."

"He doesn't even look three months old." Grace examined his tiny fingers. "But he appears clean and well cared for."

"Hello?" George called out as he came into the house. "Where is everyone?"

"In here," Grace answered. "Did you find anyone?"

George came into the room, holding up a paper sack. "I didn't see anyone out there. Not a car or anything. But I did find this bag not far from the nativity scene. It contains baby items."

"Let me see." Grace opened the bag. "It's baby clothes, diapers and baby bottles, and—"

"And the baby bottles already have milk in them," Janie announced as she pulled out a bottle. "Should we feed him now?"

"I'm not sure." Helene looked at the small glass bottle. "Why don't you go give those to Lydia for the time being, Janie? She can refrigerate them until we need them."

"And let's hold off feeding the baby for a bit." George peeled off his overcoat and leaned down to see the child better. "Let me give him a physical examination first. Just to be sure that nothing is seriously wrong with him."

"Do you think he's sick?" Grace asked quietly.

"Well, I am a doctor." He gently took the baby from Helene. "And it stands to reason that a mother in bad straits, with a sick baby . . . well, she might drop him off here to get help."

"His nose was running when I brought him inside." Helene followed George back to his office. Although he kept an office in town, he still kept an office at home as well. "But I thought it was from the cold air outside."

"He's flushed," George said as he laid the infant on his examining table. "And he feels warm to me, but I'll give him a complete checkup."

The baby was starting to cry again and Helene wasn't sure she wanted to witness the poor thing being poked and prodded. "I'll leave you to it," she told him. "Unless you need my help."

George chuckled. "I'm fairly adept at this, Helene. You go inform Lydia that dinner will be delayed. And call the police. Tell them about finding the baby."

Helene agreed, feeling uneasy as she backed out of the office. Oh, she knew the baby was in good hands with George, but she just didn't like to hear the child howling like that.

"Is the baby sick?" Janie asked with concern as Helene hung up her coat.

"I don't know. But if he is sick, he's come to the right place," Helene assured her as they returned to the front room.

"That's right," Grace said. "Grandpa can make him better."

Helene asked Grace to tell Lydia about delaying dinner, then she went to use the phone to call the police station. After identifying herself, she explained the strange situation to the sergeant who answered, then waited until Detective Albert got on the other end. "Did I hear Sergeant Smyth right? You found a baby in your manger?"

Helene quickly explained the unusual circumstances again. "And George went to look for whoever left the baby there, but he didn't see a soul. Not a car or anyone on foot. Just a bag." She described the paper sack that was left behind, and how the baby had on layers of clothing and appeared clean and well cared for.

"I haven't heard of any missing children. This sounds like a case of parental abandonment to me."

"I wondered about that." She explained George's concerns that the baby might be sick. "He's checking the baby right now."

"Even more reason for a mother to leave the child at your house. But *in the manger?*"

"He couldn't have been there long. Not more than a few minutes." She explained that they'd just put the lights on the nativity scene. "So it was very strange to find a baby there. Fortunately our dog must've seen it happen. She's the one who brought it to our attention."

"Too bad we can't question the dog."

"Yes." Helene sighed. "What should we do with the baby?"

"Well, you say it might be sick?"

"That's what George said."

"You could take it to the hospital."

Helene considered this. The poor baby had already been abandoned once. To drop it off at the hospital felt a bit heartless. "What if we just care for him for a few days?" she asked.

"Him? So it's a male baby?"

"Well, that's my assumption. He was dressed in blue, like a boy."

"Do you think you could keep him until, say, Monday?"

"Yes, I suppose we could do that." Helene knew they still had some baby furnishings in the attic. "Perhaps the mother will have second thoughts by then. And in the meantime the baby will be well cared for and George can administer any kind of medical attention it might need."

"That'd be great, Mrs. Bradley. And I must say, a baby couldn't be in better hands. The town's finest doctor as well as the chairwoman of the American Red Cross. That's a lucky lad to fall into such a fine-feathered nest."

Helene couldn't help but smile. "I hadn't considered the

Red Cross, but you're right, we are supposed to help those in need."

"You'll certainly be doing that." Now he asked her for the particulars concerning the baby's description. "Just in case we find out an infant's gone missing."

"I can't say his age for sure, but I doubt he's more than three months old. He has blondish curls and blue eyes. But then don't all babies have blue eyes? At least mine did."

"Maybe so. Any birthmarks or defects or distinguishing features?"

"Not that I have seen. In fact, he looked rather perfect. And like I said, he appears well cared for. His clothes were nice, and he was very clean. Even his little fingernails were clean and trimmed. And he's got chubby little cheeks and doesn't appear the least bit malnourished."

"Doesn't make sense, does it?"

"I suspect the mother has hit hard times."

"Sad, isn't it? A helpless baby being left like that."

"Yes . . . well, I promise we'll take excellent care of the child."

"I know you will. And I'll probably come by and do some sleuthing around in your yard and whatnot. So don't set the dog out on me."

"Goldie is a friendly dog. I don't think you need to be concerned. But we'll keep her inside."

"And I'll let you know if I turn up anything," he promised.

She thanked him, but as she hung up the phone, she almost hoped that the detective's search would be fruitless. Because something had stirred inside her the moment that she'd held that baby in her arms. It was hard to understand, but as she'd calmed and comforted the child, feeling his tiny body beginning to relax a bit, she'd experienced the tiniest glimmer of hope. A feeling she hadn't known since hearing the bad news about James.

9

Helene found their housekeeper upstairs in the master bedroom. Humming to herself and completely oblivious to the
goings-on downstairs, Velma was turning down the bed.
Helene quickly explained about their foundling.

Velma's eyebrows shot up. "Someone put a baby in the
manger?"

"Yes. Very strange. But we're going to care for the infant.
For a few days anyway. He's quite young—perhaps only two
or three months old. I'll need your help setting up a room as a
temporary nursery. I believe the crib and other nursery items
are still stored in the attic. Get Lydia to help you carry a few
things down. Just what you think we'll need until Monday."

"Want me to bring down that bassinet too—the one we
used for Janie when she was a newborn? I can set it up for
you downstairs."

"Good idea. Put it in the front room. That way we can
keep an eye on the baby when we're on the first floor."

"You know my sister Doris used to work as a baby nurse,"
Velma told her, "for the Garrets. But the children got older

so Doris doesn't work for them anymore. I could call her to see if she wants to lend a hand around here. She's a wonder with babies."

"That'd be perfect, Velma. How soon could Doris start?"

"I don't know, but I'll find out."

"Tell her George can pick her up if she needs a ride. Even tonight won't be too soon if she's available. But do tell her that the job is only a few days."

Velma nodded. "You want to use the little yellow room for the nursery?"

"Yes. With the southern exposure, it gets good sunshine." Helene thanked her. And as she went back downstairs, she sensed a bit more energy in her step. As if she suddenly had a purpose. Perhaps it was simply like she'd told the detective, she was fulfilling the mission of the American Red Cross—helping people in need. Yes, it was unconventional, but that little baby was most definitely in need.

She slipped into George's office in time to see her husband's creased brow. He was intently listening to the child's back with his stethoscope. He slowly shook his head as he moved the instrument to the baby's chest.

"How is he?" she quietly asked as George slipped the stethoscope into a pocket of his cardigan. To her relief the child was no longer crying, but he looked weak and worn out.

"Not good. I'm afraid this child is on the verge of pneumonia." He sighed. "But I don't normally give antibiotics to such a young patient."

"Oh, dear." Helene covered her mouth. "Perhaps he should be hospitalized."

George frowned grimly. "He won't get better care there than he'll get here. Especially seeing that it's a holiday weekend."

"Yes, of course, but—"

"And if necessary, I have what I need to make an oxygen tent."

"Oh, my—do you think you'll need that?"

"I don't know." George cradled the baby in his arms, peering closely into his face. "How tough are you, little man?" He paused as if waiting for a response. "How much can you take? Are you strong enough to fight off this illness on your own? Or do you need an extra boost? I just don't know." He glanced at Helene. "I don't know a thing about his medical history."

"Would it be easier to make this decision if the parents were here?"

"Certainly." George sighed. "But they're not."

"Well then, what would you do if he were *your* baby?" she asked.

"If this were my baby, I'd give him penicillin."

"Yes, of course," she said eagerly. Penicillin was being touted as the new miracle drug. "That's exactly what you should do then."

George's frown vanished. "You're right, Helene." He handed her the baby. "Thank you for helping me see it."

As George prepared penicillin, Helene relayed her conversation with the detective. "I told him we can keep the baby until Monday."

"That was generous of you." George gave the baby a shot that immediately set him to crying again. "But that's a big responsibility. Are you sure you're up for it?"

She gently rocked the fussing baby in her arms, trying to soothe him, and explained about Velma's sister. "But even if Doris can't come tonight, I can take care of him."

"And I'm sure Grace will want to lend a hand too."

"I'm not sure I want to trouble Grace. She looked so worn out when she and Janie got here the other day. I had really hoped this visit would be restful for her. She's got such a demanding life—managing Harry's business and taking care of Janie and all."

"Well, Lydia and Velma can surely take a shift of caring for him. I do think the child should be monitored throughout the night. And, of course, I'll be available if he needs additional medical help."

"I think I'll warm up one of those bottles." She spoke loudly over the baby's cries. "Maybe he's crying out of hunger."

"Good idea." He frowned again. "But be sure to sniff the bottle, Helene. Make sure it's good."

"Oh, yes. I'll definitely do that. It looked like formula. I expect that's what he's used to, but perhaps we could switch him to milk. Especially if I start him out on a mixture of half milk and half formula to get him used to it."

"You do what you think is best, but do keep the fluids flowing. And keep track of how much he is able to drink, Helene. And how much comes out the other end too."

"Maybe we should keep a chart."

"Good thinking. We'll have it ready in case the parents return. We want to show we've cared for the child in a professional way."

Although Velma's sister was unable to come that evening, Velma promised Helene that Doris would be there first thing in the morning. And Helene, still feeling strangely energized, assured everyone that she was fully capable of caring for the baby throughout the night.

"I can help you with the baby, Mom," Grace said after dinner.

"I can too," Janie said eagerly.

"And both Lydia and Velma offered to help too. If I need anyone, I'll be sure to ask." Helene leaned down to check on the baby. Tucked into the bassinet, the infant looked relatively comfortable. Although his breathing still sounded a bit raspy and his cheeks were flushed, he wasn't as agitated as before.

"He seems a little better," Grace observed.

"The medicine must be working."

"And he's not screaming," Janie said.

"Poor thing. I'm afraid he's been through a lot." Helene tucked the blanket up around him. She knew George was putting together a makeshift oxygen tent right now . . . just in case. Hopefully they wouldn't need it.

"Can we keep him, Grandma?" Janie looked up at her with hope in her eyes.

Helene smiled—and for a change this felt like a genuine smile. "We will keep him for the time being, sweetie. But hopefully his parents will realize their mistake and show up."

"What is their mistake?" Janie asked.

"Giving away their baby, silly." Grace tweaked Janie's chin. "What mommy in her right mind would give away her child?"

Helene nodded grimly. Her thoughts exactly. Perhaps the mother was *not* in her right mind. That would explain a lot.

"Maybe God sent us the baby," Janie said wistfully. "Like when God sent Baby Jesus for Christmas."

Helene and Grace exchanged looks, but said nothing.

"How's the patient?" George called out as he and Goldie came in from their after-dinner constitutional. "Resting well?"

"He appears more comfortable," Helene told him. "Do you think the penicillin might be working already?"

"It's awfully soon, but you never know. At least he's not worse." George leaned in to see the baby, checking him closely. "I've got the oxygen tent all ready to go. I'll show you how to work it when you put him to bed."

"I want to give him one more bottle before bedtime," she explained. "In about an hour or so."

"And I'd like to give him a second small dose of penicillin before I go to bed—"

"*More* penicillin?" Helene asked with concern.

"Yes, a single dose of penicillin has begun the battle against the pneumonia bacteria," George explained, "but it will take more doses to complete his treatment."

"Well, you're the doctor." Helene touched the baby's forehead. "You're in good hands, little fellow."

"And before you put him to bed, I'd like to check his temperature and listen to his lungs again."

"Can we put the baby's pajamas on now?" Janie asked hopefully. "I saw some sweet little nightgowns in that paper sack."

"Why don't you help me get him ready for bed," Helene told her granddaughter. "You get the bag and we'll go upstairs to see if Velma has his room set up yet."

"Can I help too?" Grace asked eagerly.

Helene laughed as she scooped up the infant. "Of course. We'll all get him ready for bed together." And like a tiny parade, they went up the stairs with Helene leading the way and Goldie following behind Janie.

"Look!" Janie exclaimed as they went into the small yellow bedroom. "It's a baby's room now!"

Helene glanced around, pleased to see that Velma hadn't only found appropriate baby furnishings, but she had obviously cleaned everything as well. A changing/bathing table was set against the wall with a few diapering items within easy reach. And the white crib was freshly made up with clean white sheets and a twin-sized quilt that she'd folded in half. Velma had even put a rocking chair in here.

"Very nice," Helene declared as she laid the baby on the changing table.

The baby was still wearing the little blue suit that they'd found beneath his other layers of clothing, and as Helene unbuttoned the pearl buttons, she couldn't help but admire the workmanship. "Someone sewed you a very nice little suit," she said quietly to him.

"His other clothes are well made too," Grace said as she removed some items from the bag. "Someone obviously cared about this baby."

"I think he should wear the blue nightgown," Janie declared, laying the flannel garment on the changing table.

"First he'll need a dry diaper," Helene told her. "Can you get one out of the bag, Janie? And a fresh pair of rubber pants to go over it."

"How about if I put his clothes and things in these drawers?" Grace pointed to the nearby dresser. "That'll be handy to the changing table."

"Here's a diaper, Grandma." Janie opened the folded diaper for her. "There's something inside it."

"What?" Helene glanced over to see Janie holding up a piece of paper.

"It looks like a note." Grace reached for it.

"Read it," Helene eagerly insisted as she slipped the diaper beneath the infant, securing one side with a diaper pin.

"Oh, my!" Grace sat down on the twin bed by the window.

"What? What does it say?" Helene pinned the other side, accidentally pricking the finger she had used as a buffer beneath it, but relieved she hadn't pricked the baby.

"You want me to read it aloud?" Grace asked meekly.

"Of course." Helene picked up the baby, who was starting to fuss again. With only his diaper and undershirt on, Helene held him close to her to keep him warm. She stared at her daughter. "Grace Anne? What on earth is wrong? What does the note say? Read it, please."

"It says, 'Please, take care of my baby. He is very sick and I can no longer afford to keep him.'"

"Is that all?" Helene frowned. That wasn't anything to get upset about.

"No. There's more." Grace cleared her throat and continued. "'My son's name is Jimmy. He is eight weeks old. And he's a good boy and I love him dearly. Thank you for helping him. Jimmy's Mother.'"

"His name is *Jimmy*?" Helene took in a sharp breath.

"Jimmy?" Janie echoed cheerfully. "That's a sweet name." She put her hand on Helene's elbow. "Don't you like that name, Grandma?"

"Yes, yes, I do like that name." Helene turned back to the changing table and, laying Jimmy back down, she slipped the soft flannel nightgown over his head, fastening the snaps at the neckline then pulling the drawstring at the bottom of the garment to turn the nightgown into a sleep sack that would keep his feet warm.

"You see, we used to call Uncle James by that name," Grace explained to Janie. "When he was little we called him Jimmy. After he got bigger, he didn't like going by Jimmy. He went by James instead. Some of his friends called him Jim."

"Maybe Uncle James sent us Jimmy," Janie declared with enthusiasm. "From *heaven*. Just like when Baby Jesus came from heaven."

Once again, Helene and Grace exchanged uncomfortable glances. Some childish conclusions were just too hard to respond to in an honest manner.

"Well, we will take care of this little Jimmy just as if Uncle James *had* sent him from heaven," Helene finally declared. She held the baby for Janie to see. "How does he look in his little nightgown?"

Janie reached out to touch the baby's cheek. "Jimmy, you are very sweet."

With Jimmy starting to fuss again, Helene sat down in

the rocking chair, hoping to soothe him . . . and herself. As strange as it seemed, maybe Janie was right. Maybe God really had sent them this baby.

***

Helene had just finished Jimmy's three a.m. feeding and, to her relief, the infant was breathing more easily. So far she had no need of George's makeshift oxygen tent. Nor had she felt compelled to wake her husband. She was also relieved that the half-and-half mixture of cow's milk and formula hadn't bothered little Jimmy's tummy. She'd found it disturbing that so many young mothers had taken to using these store-bought baby formulas. She knew it was convenient for working mothers. Especially since so many women had joined the workforce with their men off at war. But, according to George, formula milk wasn't nearly as nutritious as mother's milk—and he still believed cow's milk was superior to formula as well.

She continued rocking Jimmy until she felt certain he was soundly asleep, then gently laid him on his side in the crib— the same way she had always put her own babies to sleep. Had it been more than two decades since she had been a young mother? She felt as if it all instantly had come back to her. So much so that she could imagine herself becoming a mommy to little Jimmy.

Climbing back into the narrow twin bed, Helene wondered again at what Janie had said. Maybe the child was right. Maybe God *had* given them this baby . . . perhaps as a replacement for her own lost son. Oh, she knew the child hadn't been literally dropped down from heaven like Janie believed. But the circumstances that had delivered the baby into their manger might have been directed by God. In this twilight hour, she felt that was entirely possible. And suddenly she felt her heart growing warmer toward a God who could work such a miracle.

As Helene turned off the bedside light, she realized that she had been angry at God for months now—ever since receiving that awful telegram about James last spring. Certainly, it wasn't a rage she'd ever expressed openly. But even while seated at church, it would be simmering inside of her. Perhaps caring for this helpless infant would allow her to let go of her fury. It was obvious that the child needed someone to care for him. He'd been in dire straits when they'd taken him in and already he was doing better.

Having Baby Jimmy to care for made it much easier to tell Grace and Janie goodbye. But it had the opposite effect on little Janie. "I don't want to leave him," she complained as George carried their bags out to their car. "He's so sweet and cute." Janie reached up to touch the infant's cheek. "And his skin is so soft."

"Well, we have to go home," Grace firmly told Janie. "I have work and you have kindergarten. Remember?"

"Will Baby Jimmy still be here when we come back for Christmas?" Janie asked Helene.

Helene grimaced. "I, uh, I don't know. He might have to—"

"What if I never see him again?" Janie looked close to tears. "You have to keep him, Grandma. God put him in our manger so that you could keep him."

George knelt down in front of Janie, looking intently into her face. "We don't really know that for sure, sweetheart. But we do know that no matter what happens with Jimmy, he will be lovingly cared for. Just like you are." He kissed her cheek. "And just think—in a few weeks you and your mommy will be back here for Christmas."

"And Daddy might be here too," Grace announced.

"Daddy's coming home! Daddy's coming home!" Suddenly Janie was dancing about the driveway, her sorrow over not seeing Jimmy again replaced by exuberance.

"Really?" George stood. "Harry has leave at Christmastime?"

Grace smiled sheepishly at her parents. "Well, it was supposed to be a secret—and it's not a hundred percent for sure—but I think so."

Even if it was a smoke screen to distract Janie from fretting over Baby Jimmy, Helene was grateful for this news as she kissed them both goodbye. And, to her surprise, she no longer felt so angry at Harry for the role he'd played in enticing her son into the wide blue yonder. Truth be told, James had always been a strong-willed and adventuresome boy. It was no wonder he'd taken to the skies like he had. Perhaps it was time for her to move on . . . forgive and forget. Perhaps this baby would help her to do so. Bundling him closer to her, she waved to Grace and Janie as their car pulled away, then hurried back into the warmth of the house.

She felt confident, thanks to George's medical expertise and her maternal skills, this child's health would greatly improve in the next few days. She could just imagine the baby with a healthy glow, giggling and happy. Like Detective Albert had said, the child had "fallen into a fine-feathered nest." And based on the note penned by Jimmy's mother, Helene was certain the desperate woman must've specifically picked George and Helene for this task. Helene wondered about the mother . . . was she someone they knew? Perhaps someone from church? Or one of George's patients? Helene's best guess was that the mother was young. Perhaps an adolescent who had found herself in trouble . . . or perhaps someone trapped in poverty. Maybe even from the nearby reservation—although the child's fair looks suggested otherwise. In fact, with Helene's light brown hair and blue eyes, it wouldn't be difficult to pass little Jimmy off as her own.

She wondered what George would say to the idea of them becoming parents again. Even though he was nearly sixty and planning for retirement in the next few years, Helene was only forty-eight. It was unusual, but she'd heard of women her age having babies. And George, despite his years, was young at heart. In her opinion, they would make fine parents to a young child. She felt certain that Jimmy's mother would agree.

=== 10 ===

George felt torn as he walked to town on Monday morning. On one hand, he was thrilled to see Helene back to her old self. In fact, it was even better than that—he hadn't seen his wife this happy in years. Not since before the war. Having a baby in the house just brought out the best in her. She wasn't even depressed like she usually would be after Grace and Janie went home. It was refreshing.

But on the other hand, Jimmy was not their baby. And each additional day spent caring for the child would only make it harder for Helene to let him go.

"Good morning, Dr. Bradley." Betty took his coat and hat for him, putting them in the closet. "Cora won't be in until ten today. She had to take her mother to the train station. But I'll cover for her." She smiled. "Did you have a good Thanksgiving?"

"Well, it was interesting anyway." He quickly told Betty about finding a baby in the manger on Friday. She had been his nurse since he'd first opened this clinic and was almost like family.

"My goodness!"

"Helene has already grown quite fond of him." He grimaced. "The child's name is Jimmy."

Betty had been an Army nurse in the First World War and was usually unflappable, but she looked genuinely stunned now. "How very, very odd."

He nodded grimly. "Janie insisted that the baby had been sent to us by God. Just like Baby Jesus. And that's why he was in the manger."

"Oh, my." Betty chuckled. "That little Janie is a clever one."

He tapped the appointment book on Cora's desk. "When is my first patient?"

"Not until eleven. But after that you'll be busy most of the afternoon."

George sat on the edge of the reception desk—something he wouldn't dare do if Cora was here. Folding his arms in front of him, he let out a long sigh. "Helene is really hoping that we can keep the baby, Betty."

"Oh . . . ?"

"She's like a new woman. I haven't seen her this happy since . . . well, it's been a long time."

"Bless her heart. Losing James has been very hard on her . . . well, on both of you." She sighed. "On everyone . . ."

He just nodded.

"How do you feel about it? I mean, keeping the child."

He pursed his lips. "Honestly?"

"Of course."

"Well, I'll be sixty next year and I'd really been looking

forward to retirement. I had hoped that Helene and I might do some traveling—well, if this blasted war ever ends."

"So you're not terribly interested in raising a second family?"

"Not really." He frowned. "But I can't tell Helene. Honestly, Betty, she is over the moon for this child. I heard her singing to him this morning." He shook his head. "And now she is convinced that little Jimmy resembles James—when he was an infant."

"Does he?"

George shrugged as he stood up. "You know me, Betty. All babies look alike."

She smiled.

He explained about how sick the baby was when they took him in. "But I gave him penicillin and he's much better. He's responding like a sturdy little lad."

"Where do you suppose he came from? Who left him there?"

"That's what I intend to find out." He glanced at the wall clock. "You say I've no appointments until eleven?"

"That's right."

"Maybe I'll do some sleuthing." He went back to the closet and retrieved his overcoat and hat. "Do you recall any patients that I've cared for in the past? Any young women that might've found themselves in a difficult position? With child?"

"I can't think of any offhand, and the only baby you've delivered in the past three months was a girl. But I can go over our files and see if there's a woman that might've found herself in trouble like that." She held up a finger. "And Harvey might know something."

"Good idea. Ask Harvey." Betty's husband taught science

at the high school. "I think I'll run by the police station and have a conversation with Detective Albert. See if he's discovered anything."

"Good luck."

George thanked her, but as he went outside he wondered what "good luck" really would be in this situation. Helene's idea of good luck would be never to find the mother and simply raise the child as their own. He knew he should be supportive of this—especially considering how much happier she'd been these past couple of days. He was amazed and impressed how easily she'd slipped into the role of mother. And, as she'd pointed out, some women her age had babies. After all, hadn't he just delivered one with Ida Adams last year? And their family was doing just fine. "It will keep me younger," she'd assured him this morning. And he had to admit that having Doris with them, as the baby's nursemaid, certainly lightened the load. But, really, did he want to raise a child . . . at his age?

Detective Albert was happy to see George. "I was just about to call you," he said as he led George into his office. "I think I might've discovered the identity of the mystery mother."

"Really?" George removed his hat as he sat down.

"Well, some of the pieces fit. But not everything."

"Tell me about it."

"A young woman came to town last week. She'd been staying at the Wallace Hotel. And, according to Bill Jones, the manager, this woman had a baby."

"Yes?" George leaned forward.

"The young woman was from California. Her name is Amelia Richards. Nice-looking woman, but Bill suspected she was down on her luck."

"What do you mean? How would he know?"

"Apparently she was short on funds. She told Bill she wanted to get a job, but that she needed to have the room on credit for a week or so."

"Oh?"

"Of course, Bill couldn't give it to her. So she checked out on Sunday."

"Where did she go?"

"I don't know." Detective Albert frowned. "This is where it doesn't quite make sense."

"What?"

"Bill said she had her baby with her when she left."

"On Sunday?"

The detective nodded glumly.

"Then she can't be the mother we're looking for."

"But that's the only lead I had that made sense. A lone woman shows up in Rockford with an infant. Down on her luck. And you find an abandoned baby in your manger."

"But Bill saw her leave with the baby?" George considered this. "Did you question him carefully? Was he certain that it was Sunday?"

"He showed me his book."

"And he saw the baby with her? On Sunday?"

"That's right."

George suddenly stood. "But what if the baby wasn't a baby?"

"What are you talking about?"

"There was a doll in the manger—and the doll went missing!"

Detective Albert stood up quickly. "Are you thinking what I'm thinking?"

"I'm thinking we need to talk to Bill."

Before long they were quizzing Bill about the baby that Amelia Richards had departed with the day before.

"Now that I think of it, I suppose it could've been a doll. She had it bundled up . . . so I couldn't see its face. And, come to think of it, I didn't get any complaints about noise from the baby during the weekend. I had to move a guest to a different room on Thanksgiving because the baby's cries had disturbed them the night before. And my daughter Dorothy had been doing some babysitting for Mrs. Richards, but she never got another call after Friday."

"Do you know where Mrs. Richards went after she left here yesterday?" George pressed.

Bill shook his head no. "I assumed it was to the train station."

"But you told me she wanted to get a job," Detective Albert pressed. "Any idea where she planned to work?"

He shook his head again.

"Do you think your daughter might know?" George asked. "Since she worked for Mrs. Richards?"

"She might. But she's in school until three."

"And you say Mrs. Richards came out from California?" George asked him.

"Yep. Her and the baby came here on the train. I remember

she mentioned it. That's why I figured she probably left on the train too."

Detective Albert made some notes. "I'll check with the train station. And then I'll question Dorothy later this afternoon." He looked hopefully at George. "We'll find her."

"I sure hope so."

As George walked back to the clinic, he prayed a silent prayer for Amelia Richards. He felt truly sorry for the young woman. Like Helene had pointed out more than once, little Jimmy appeared well cared for. Other than being so ill, the child had been properly fed and clothed. Whoever this Amelia Richards was, she was not a negligent mother. Well, aside from the abandonment issue. But if she was unable to afford more nights at the Wallace Hotel, which wasn't too expensive, she had to be down on her luck. So he prayed for her welfare and he prayed that God would help them to find her.

"There you are," Cora said eagerly as George came into the clinic. "Sally Peterson just called. She works at Beulah's Beauty Shop. She took in a new roommate, but the woman has become quite ill. She wondered if you could make a house call."

George pointed up at the clock. "My first appointment should be here soon and Betty told me I would be busy all afternoon. I probably can't get away until after—"

"Sally said this woman is desperately ill. She thinks it might be pneumonia."

George frowned . . . wondering if it could possibly be. "Did you get the name of the woman—I mean, the one who is sick?"

Cora looked down at her notepad. "Amelia something. I didn't catch the last name. But she's at Sally Peterson's and Sally lives in the apartment above Beulah's—"

"Call Sally back and tell her I'm on my way." He hurried to his office, nearly running over Betty in the hallway. "You take care of the eleven o'clock appointment until I get back," he ordered.

"Back from where?" She followed him into his office, waiting as he checked his doctor bag, making sure he had what he would need.

"I think we found her, Betty. The mother of the baby!"

11

"You were right to call me," George told Sally after he finished a preliminary exam of the frail blonde woman on the sleeper sofa. "May I use your phone?"

"Yes, of course." Sally pointed to the little telephone table by the door. "It's a party line to the beauty shop downstairs. Hopefully no one's on the other end." She glanced at her watch. "In fact, if you don't need me, I should go down there. I have a lady scheduled for a permanent wave waiting for me."

"Go ahead," he said as he dialed the hospital's phone number. "I'm going to arrange for a transport to Saint Joseph's."

Sally's brows arched. "But Amelia doesn't have a cent, Dr. Bradley. She can't afford to—"

"It'll be covered," he assured her.

Sally left, and George quickly explained the situation to the hospital nurse, requesting both an ambulance and a private room. "Make sure the ambulance is carrying oxygen. We'll need an oxygen tent set up and ready at the hospital. And an IV," he told her. "I'll be arriving and attending the patient and her condition is critical."

As he waited for the ambulance to get there, he called his office, explaining to Cora that this was an emergency and to reschedule his appointments for the next two hours. Finally, he sat down on the chair by the sofa, gazing down at the young woman. Despite the effects of her illness, he could see she was very attractive. But he could also see she was hanging onto her life by a fragile thread.

"Can you hear me, Mrs. Richards?" He spoke loudly because so far she'd been incoherent. Even when he'd administered a shot of penicillin she had barely flinched. But now she nodded slightly. "Don't try to speak," he said gently. "We're going to transport you to Saint Joseph Hospital. I've made all the arrangements. I'll be taking care of you. My name is Dr. Bradley."

As soon as he said his name, her blue eyes fluttered open. For a brief moment they met his, and then with a raspy sigh she closed them again, lying so deathly still that he checked her pulse to be sure she was still alive. For the second time today, George said a prayer for this woman. Then, hearing the whine of the ambulance siren, he went outside to wave at the medical staff, guiding them up to the apartment.

George held her hand as they traveled in the back of the ambulance. Before long, she was being settled into a private room where, according to his instructions, an oxygen tent and IV were prepared and ready.

George did everything he could for the young woman and then, knowing she was in good hands with the medical staff, he returned to his clinic. But his steps were heavy as he went inside. The young woman's life was hanging in the balance, and despite the good medical attention she would be receiving, it would be touch and go for the next few days. To his relief, no patients were in his waiting room.

"I cleared your schedule until two o'clock," Cora informed him.

"Thank you." He removed his hat.

"How is she?" Betty asked with concern.

"Not good," he confessed, starting to unbutton his overcoat.

"Betty told me about the baby in your manger," Cora declared. "Is that woman really the mother?"

"I believe so."

"Did she tell you why she abandoned her baby?" Cora asked eagerly.

"No . . . She's in bad shape. Pneumonia. She can barely speak."

"The poor thing."

He just nodded.

"You don't need to be here until two," Cora reminded him. "Maybe you should go home and have your lunch."

"Yes," Betty agreed. "Go put your feet up awhile. You've already had a busy morning."

George didn't argue with them. As he walked the few blocks toward home, he couldn't remember when he'd felt this tired. His feet felt like lead. Maybe the years were catching up with him faster than he realized. His own father had been only sixty-two when he'd passed away. What if George was to follow in his footsteps? And, really, how could a man of his age possibly consider becoming a father to an infant son. It just wasn't fair. Not to any of them. For the third time today he prayed for the young woman. This time he pleaded with God to help Amelia Richards to get well—well enough to care for her own child.

"You're home," Helene happily announced as George came into the front room. "I didn't expect you for lunch." She paused from draping a strand of gold Christmas tinsel across the fireplace mantel.

"That looks pretty," George said.

"Well, having a baby around has put me in a Christmassy mood." She smiled as she came over to greet and kiss him. "Let me take your coat and hat, and then I'll go tell Lydia to get some lunch started."

"Thanks, dear." He considered telling her about his morning as she helped him out of his coat, but she was in such good spirits, he hated to spoil it. And he knew that this news would. He went over to peer into the bassinet by Helene's favorite armchair. The baby was sleeping peacefully. "How's our little houseguest doing?"

"Just fine. He's so much better, George. You made the right decision in giving him those antibiotics. They've really done the trick."

"Well, his case was probably not as advanced as . . . as I thought." He refrained from saying "as advanced as his mother's." While Helene went to find Lydia, George studied the sleeping infant. It was strange to think that the young woman lying in the oxygen tent was this child's mother. Strange and sad.

"Lydia said it'll take her about fifteen minutes to whip up something good. Do you have that long?"

"That's fine." He nodded to Helene's chair. "Why don't you sit down, dear."

She gave him an uncertain look.

"Please," he insisted. "There's something I need to tell you."

"Oh?" She eased herself into her chair, watching him cautiously. "Why don't you sit down too?"

He sat across from her, nervously folding his hands in his lap. "I've had an interesting morning, Helene." Now he explained about meeting with Detective Albert and going to the hotel and finally about tending to the sick young woman. "We don't know this for certain, but Detective Albert thinks that Amelia Richards is the baby's mother."

"Jimmy's mother?" she said weakly.

He simply nodded.

"What does this mean?"

"I'm not sure," he admitted. "The young woman is in a very bad way, Helene."

"Really?" Her expression was hard to read.

"She's getting the best care possible, but her condition is critical."

"Oh . . . Do you think she'll pull through?"

"To be honest, I'd give her about fifty-fifty odds right now. And that's probably optimistic."

Helene frowned. "Well, of course, I'm terribly sad for this poor woman, George. But does this mean we may get to keep Jimmy?"

He wrung his hands and stared down at the carpet. "I don't know."

"Because if she's in such a bad way, she would probably be relieved to know that we want to keep her baby . . . that we love him . . . and that we would bring him up in the best way possible. Wouldn't that be a comfort to her?"

"I suppose."

Her eyes brightened. "Could I go and speak with her, George?"

"Not today. And not likely tomorrow. She's not well enough to have visitors or to speak to anyone yet. Not until she's out of the woods."

"But as soon as she can have visitors, I'd like to go, George. I know how a mother thinks. I know she must be so worried about her child. I want to reassure her that he's really in good hands—and that his health is greatly improved."

"Yes, that is a good idea," he conceded. "Perhaps I can convey that information to her."

"Yes," she said eagerly. "Promise me that you'll do that, George."

"I promise. And I already planned to go check in on her after my last appointment today."

"Oh, good." She nodded. "That makes me feel better."

"So plan on a late dinner. Maybe around eight."

"That's fine." And now the baby began to wake up and Helene, distracted with caring for the infant, appeared to forget all about the child's mother.

It was close to six by the time George made it back to the hospital and, bracing himself for bad news, stopped by the nurses' station to inquire about his patient. "Her condition hasn't changed much," the head nurse informed him. "But at least she's not worsened."

"Yes, that's something. Thank you, Nurse Crawford. And I didn't mention it earlier, but I want to be notified if there is any change in her condition—for better or worse. Since the young woman appears to have no family in town, we will act as her next of kin."

Nurse Crawford nodded solemnly. "I see."

He thanked her again and went to check on Amelia. As he examined her vitals, he had to concur with Nurse Crawford. Mrs. Richards's condition was much the same, although she did appear to be resting a bit better. That was something. He was about to take his leave when he remembered what Helene had asked him to do. In fact, hadn't he promised her that he would say something?

He put his stethoscope away, then took the chair by her bedside, trying to think of the best words to say—and wondering if she was even conscious and able to hear him. "Mrs. Richards," he spoke clearly as he took her hand. "Are you awake? If you can hear me, just give my fingers a little squeeze." Feeling a slight squeeze, he continued. "You left your child at my home last week. And I promised my wife that I would tell you that little Jimmy is doing just fine. He is much better. On the road to recovery. Do you understand what I'm saying? Just squeeze my fingers if you do." She made another weak squeeze.

"Oh, good." He sighed. "My wife will be relieved to hear this. She is quite smitten by your little lad," he continued, rambling. "Such a fine-looking baby. My wife feels that he's had very good care. And she is giving him very good care herself." He went on to tell her about how they'd hired a baby nurse named Doris and how she was quite fond of Jimmy too. "So, all in all, your child is in very good hands. The only thing you need to think about is getting well. Just rest and get better, Mrs. Richards. Don't worry about a single thing. You and your little boy are both in good hands."

Now, for the fourth time today, George prayed for Amelia Richards. Only this time, he prayed the words aloud. "Dear Heavenly Father," he began slowly, "please, take care of your child Amelia Richards. Help her to get healthy and well so that she can, once again, be a fine mother for her little boy. Amen." He felt a light squeeze on his fingers, almost as if she was agreeing with his prayer.

"Now do as your doctor has ordered," he gently said as he stood. "Just rest and get stronger and do not worry about your child. Little Jimmy is perfectly fine. And I will be back here to see you in the morning."

Hopefully Amelia Richards would still be in the land of the living by morning. At the moment, he couldn't be certain. If she didn't make it, at least he had kept his promise to Helene—and he thought the young mother had understood his words. Still, everything inside of him desperately hoped that she would make it.

12

A full week had passed before Amelia was strong enough to have the oxygen tent removed from her room. Even then, George was uncertain. On one hand, he didn't like to leave a patient on oxygen any longer than necessary. On the other hand, he didn't want to see her slightly improved condition deteriorate for lack of oxygen. It was not an easy call. But after a couple of days, seeing the young mother sitting up in her bed, sipping clear chicken broth for her lunch, he knew he'd made the right decision.

"How are you feeling tonight?" he asked that same evening. He was performing his usual exam, checking her lungs and heart and blood pressure—which had all improved remarkably.

"Much better," she said quietly. "I'm so grateful . . . for everything, Dr. Bradley. How can I ever thank—"

"Never mind that." He waved his hand. "You've thanked me over and over, Mrs. Richards."

"Amelia," she gently corrected him. She'd already asked him to call her by her first name—more than once.

111

"Yes . . . Amelia. And a fine name too." As he closed his doctor's bag, he decided that she was probably strong enough for a short conversation. "Do you mind if I sit for a spell?"

"Not at all." She nodded to the nearby chair.

"Jimmy is doing just fine," he told her, knowing that would've been the first question from her lips. "Helene said he's even gained some weight." He wouldn't tell her what else Helene had been saying of late. The poor woman. As relieved as Helene was that Amelia was recovering, she was frantically worried that meant that Amelia would take her son back. George was caught in the middle.

Amelia smiled, but her eyes were sad. "I miss Jimmy so much."

"That is exactly why you're working so hard at getting well, Amelia."

She nodded somberly.

George let out a long sigh. "I don't want to wear you out, but I do have some questions. Do you feel strong enough?"

Again, she nodded, but her brow was creased and he knew she was uneasy.

"I know you're from California, right?"

"Right. San Diego."

"Do you have family there?"

"Not really . . ." She frowned. "I have a mother and stepfather, but we are not on good terms."

"I see." He pursed his lips. "And, uh, does Jimmy have a father in San Diego?"

"Jimmy's father was killed in the war."

George felt a small wave of relief. He wasn't even sure

why exactly. Perhaps it was simply easier to think of Amelia as a war widow. "I'm sorry for your loss," he told her. "It must be difficult bringing up a child on your own. Particularly without family to help." He rubbed his chin. "But I am curious, Amelia, what made you leave San Diego to come here? I assume you have no family here. And Rockford is . . . well, it must be quite a change from San Diego." He studied her closely now, watching as her clear blue eyes grew moist with tears.

"I, uh, I came here for Jimmy's sake," she said quietly.

"I don't understand."

"Jimmy has family here."

A strange, almost electrical rush ran through George at these words—and somehow he knew exactly what she was saying. Yet surely it was impossible.

"Your son and I had planned to get married," she said a bit breathlessly. "James had filled out the marriage license, and we were going in the next day. But he got called back to the ship that evening." Tears were pouring down her cheeks now. "And, well, we knew he was going into active duty and—" She collapsed into sobs and George was so shocked that he was literally speechless. Instead of saying a single word, he got out of the chair, wrapped his arms around her, and simply held her in the same way he would hold his own daughter.

"There, there," he finally said. "It will be okay, Amelia. Everything will be okay." But now she was starting to wheeze and cough again and he knew these tumultuous emotions were not helping her condition. If he'd had any clue that her story was so complicated and difficult, he wouldn't have made his inquiries.

"Lean back." He fluffed the pillows behind her. "Take a slow, deep breath and try to relax."

She leaned back, but between her tears and the wheezing, he knew that she needed help. He gave her a mild tranquilizer, then went to find the head nurse, requesting the oxygen tent once more. "Just for the night," he explained. "That patient is in some distress."

As George helped the orderly get the oxygen tent arranged, he was still trying to absorb what Amelia had just confessed. A part of him was not too surprised—it was as if he had instinctively known something like this. But the other part of him was stunned beyond words. He was full of questions, but he knew his questions would have to wait until she was stronger. In the meantime, he had to break this shocking news to his wife. Poor Helene! He had no idea how she would respond. The baby that she'd been caring for and bonding with—even hoping to adopt as her own— was really her grandchild? It was more than he could take in—how would Helene possibly handle it? How would he tell her?

After a sleepless night, George knew that he had to tell Helene the truth about Amelia. It wouldn't be easy, but it had to be done. After an uncomfortably quiet evening, Helene had become suspicious that something was troubling him. But he had blamed it on a busy day and being tired.

Now, as he paced back and forth in his office downstairs, he knew what he needed to do. Hearing the baby upstairs, he suddenly wanted a good look at the child. Last night, Jimmy had already been put to bed by the time George got home.

Tiptoeing up the stairs, George found Doris just getting ready to give Jimmy a bottle. "May I?" George asked, holding out his hands.

"You want to feed the baby?"

"I do." He nodded.

She shrugged. "Well, I guess you should know how to do it . . . being a doctor and all." She handed him the child and then the bottle. "I'll just leave you to it then."

As she left the room, George sat down in the rocker. Cradling the squirming infant in his arms, he stuck the warmed bottle in the baby's mouth, then watched with great interest as Jimmy vigorously sucked on it. Although George had always claimed that all babies looked alike, he could see something uniquely familiar in this one. He had no reason to doubt Amelia's story.

"What on earth are you doing?" Helene asked in wonder as she came into the nursery, still wearing her dressing gown.

"Feeding the baby," he answered nonchalantly.

"I can see that, George. But where's Doris and why are you—"

"Because I wanted to," he declared. "I wanted a good look at the little feller."

Helene smiled. "He is sweet, isn't he?"

"He's a fine specimen of a baby."

"Oh, you don't have to sound so clinical, George." She sat down on the edge of the twin bed. "He's absolutely perfect."

"Does he still remind you of James? I mean, when James was an infant?"

"He really does, George. Can you see it too?"

Feeling a slight lump in his throat, George just nodded. Looking down into the baby's ocean-blue eyes . . . it was almost like seeing James—and bittersweet.

"I'm so glad you think so too. Because I've been giving this dilemma a lot of thought these past couple of days, George. I'm very happy that Amelia is getting better. But she is in no position to raise a child. She obviously doesn't have a penny to her name. And she appears to have no husband or family. I think she made a very wise decision to put Jimmy in our care, and that is why I think we should offer to adopt him. That way she can have a fresh start in her life. In fact, I'd even like to help her out financially. We'll give her train fare to California and enough money to live on until she's strong enough to get a job. And as soon as you give me the go-ahead, I will visit her in the hospital and discuss this—"

"Stop it." George looked intently at her.

"What?" Helene's brow creased.

"You do not understand the whole situation."

"Well, of course not. But I do understand that Jimmy needs a good stable home, George. And that's something we can—"

"Listen to me, Helene," he said with quiet intensity. "There is a reason that Amelia left San Diego to come here. A reason

116

she decided to leave Jimmy with us. I'm surprised you haven't guessed it yourself."

"What?" She tilted her head to one side.

"Jimmy is your grandson, Helene. He is James's child."

Helene's face grew visibly pale. So much so that George wondered if she were about to faint. "Wh-what?" she asked in a tiny voice.

"Amelia and James were about to be married. He was called back to the ship before they could wed. That's when he left for the Pacific that last time. And she had his baby."

"No." Helene firmly shook her head. "That's not possible."

George sighed. "Of course, it's possible. I've even done the math. Remember how James had leave in San Diego at Christmastime."

"Yes, he was going to come home . . . but he didn't."

"Probably because he'd met Amelia around that time. And then he got called back to the ship early. Remember he called us shortly before shipping out. Shortly after New Year's. Our conversation was cut short, but he even said that he had some good news to share. Remember, Helene?"

"That still doesn't make it so, George. I can't believe that James would be involved like that. He wouldn't do anything dishonorable, George. Leave a girl in that condition. Not my son."

"Oh, Helene." George sighed.

"This girl made up that story." Helene stood with clenched fists. "She thinks we have money—that she can get something from us."

"No, that's not—"

"We've been set up, George. Lured in. She's using her baby to get to us."

"That's crazy, Helene." George looked down at Jimmy. He was done with the bottle, which probably meant he needed to be burped. So, trying to act more experienced than he felt, George lifted the baby to his left shoulder as he slowly stood and gently patted him on the back. "I happen to believe Amelia," he calmly told his wife. "She nearly died from pneumonia. She would have no reason to make up such a story. It all makes sense. It adds up just right."

"Except that it's all wrong," she insisted.

"Why would you say that?" George continued to pat the baby's back. "Aren't you delighted to think that we have James's baby right here with us? It's almost like having—"

"It's *not* James's baby," she said stubbornly. "James would *not* do something like that. I'm his mother. I know my own son. This is wrong. All wrong!" And just as she stormed out of the nursery, Jimmy spit up all over George's favorite wool cardigan.

"Oh, dear," Doris said when she found George trying to wipe his sweater with a diaper. "You go clean yourself up, and I'll take care of the little one."

As George went to change his clothes, he tried to make heads or tails of his wife. He had imagined various reactions from her, but he felt completely blindsided by this one. How could she be so absolutely certain that James was not Jimmy's father? After all, James had been a healthy young man. Attractive to the females. And after flying as a Navy pilot these past few years, he had undoubtedly changed in some ways. George was aware that James enjoyed an occasional beer. That he'd taken up cigarette smoking—something that Helene abhorred. Why was it so hard for her to accept that it was possible that James had fathered a child as well?

13

Amelia watched as a junior nurse taped the end of some shiny green Christmas tinsel to one side of the window, then gracefully draped the strand across to the other side. Next she hung several sparkling glass Christmas balls on the strand. "How's that?" the young volunteer asked.

"Very pretty," Amelia told her. "Thank you for making my room more cheery."

"You're welcome." The girl came over to her bed. "I heard you might get to go home before long."

Amelia forced a smile, not caring to admit that she actually had no *home* to go to. "Yes, I hope to be released soon," she told the girl. "Perhaps even by the end of the week." Home or no home, she would be glad to escape this hospital. Not that she hadn't been treated properly. In fact, she couldn't remember having been so well cared for—ever. Still, it felt awkward being an "invalid." Every day she was working to get stronger—walking up and down the hall as well as doing her breathing exercises. She felt that she was ready to be released. But she'd learned not to argue with Dr. Bradley.

"Christmas is less than two weeks away," the junior nurse said as she straightened the cover on Amelia's bed. "I heard it will be a white Christmas too. In fact, the radio said we might get snow by the end of the week."

Amelia looked out the window, trying to imagine what it would look like with fresh white snow all over this town. "That would be nice."

"Hello?"

Amelia looked up to see an attractive older woman standing in her doorway. She had on a gray fur coat and pretty hat. "Yes?" Amelia studied the woman closely and realized this was James's mother. They had the same coloring, same straight nose and strong chin. Plus Dr. Bradley had warned her just yesterday that his wife planned to visit. He'd also explained how Mrs. Bradley was having difficulty accepting the truth that Jimmy was actually her grandson. "Actually, that's an understatement," he'd confessed. "So don't be surprised if she questions you about this." Amelia had assured him that wouldn't be a problem and that she had, in fact, expected something like this.

"Amelia Richards?" The woman tugged on her pale gray gloves.

Amelia nodded. "You must be Mrs. Bradley."

"That's right." She remained in the doorway with a hard-to-read expression.

"Please, come in." Amelia waved toward the nearby chair.

"Excuse me," the junior nurse said in a nervous-sounding voice. "I'll leave you with your guest."

"Close the door on your way out," Mrs. Bradley instructed the girl.

Amelia watched as Mrs. Bradley slowly removed her luxurious wrap, laying it over the back of her chair before she sat down. "I'm sure you know why I'm here." Mrs. Bradley began to peel off her fine leather gloves.

"I want to thank you"—Amelia pulled the coverlet higher, sitting up straighter in bed and inserting pleasantness into her voice—"for taking such excellent care of Jimmy. I've asked Dr. Bradley to convey my gratitude, but I've been eager to meet you and tell you personally. I know I can never repay you, but I—"

"No need to repay me." She stiffly waved her hand.

"Well, it's taken a load off my mind." Amelia forced an uneasy smile. "How is he doing?"

"Jimmy is much better. Quite well. He has even gained several ounces since he's been in our care. I weigh him daily to be sure."

"Oh, good." Amelia felt a mixture of relief and guilt. She felt delighted that Jimmy's health was improved, but terrible that he'd gotten so ill during her watch. Perhaps she truly was an unfit mother.

"So . . . let me get to the point, Miss Richards. Dr. Bradley tells me that you claim to have been involved with our son—that Jimmy is James's child."

"That's true." Amelia could feel her hands trembling as she clutched the edge of the coverlet.

"Well, I do not want to offend you, Miss Richards, but that is preposterous."

Amelia stared at her hands, struggling to think of the right words—some way to convince James's mother of the truth . . . or perhaps it didn't really matter.

"I *know* my son, Miss Richards, and I *know* he couldn't possibly be the father of your child. That sort of behavior is completely out of character for my son. Perhaps you were involved with another man by the name of James Bradley. I suspect it is not an uncommon name. But I feel certain that my deceased son is not the father of your baby."

Amelia looked up at her. "I'm sorry, Mrs. Bradley . . . sorry that this is so disturbing to you. But it is the truth. And I'm also sorry that James and I did not have time to get properly married like we had planned to do . . . like we should've done."

Mrs. Bradley cleared her throat, glancing toward the door as if worried that someone might come in.

"If it would make you feel better, I can show you the marriage license application that James filled out for us. Perhaps that would convince you that I'm telling you the truth."

"Do you have that document here, Miss Richards?"

"Please," she pleaded, "call me Amelia."

Mrs. Bradley shrugged. "Fine. *Amelia.* Did you bring the marriage license application with you?"

"It's in my suitcase. In Sally's apartment above the beauty shop."

"Never mind." Mrs. Bradley waved a dismissive hand. "As I said, there are probably numerous young servicemen by that same name. Besides, it's entirely possible that a person might counterfeit a document like that."

"But what about facts like birth dates and birthplaces and—"

"Those facts are easily found and duplicated. Even if you produced such a document, how would I know it was authentic?" Her eyes narrowed with what looked like suspicion.

Suppressing the urge to hotly defend herself, Amelia weighed her response. After all, this was the woman caring for her child . . . and James's mother. "But wouldn't you recognize your own son's handwriting?"

Mrs. Bradley's brow creased as she pursed her lips, saying nothing for a long moment.

"Perhaps I could call Sally and ask her to—"

"What do you want, Amelia?" Her tone grew urgent. "Why are you here?"

"What do you mean?" She looked around the private room. "I was hospitalized because I—"

"*Why* are you here? In Rockford? *Why* did you abandon your baby with us?" The intensity of her stare was disturbing. "What exactly are you after? Do you think you can blackmail us for some kind of settlement?"

"No . . ." Amelia took in a slow breath, trying to remain calm. "I came to Rockford simply because I wanted Jimmy to meet his grandparents." But she knew that wasn't the whole truth. She had wanted to meet James's parents too. She had wanted them to accept her . . . perhaps to even make her part of the family. Not to live with them, but simply to have a connection. In some ways Dr. Bradley had treated her like family. But she knew this woman never would. Suddenly Amelia remembered what she'd heard at Beulah's Beauty

Shop that first day—the cold, hard portrait the ladies had painted of Mrs. Bradley blossomed to life. It was hopeless.

"Let's pretend for a moment that what you're saying is true." Mrs. Bradley spoke quietly, but the words were laced with insincerity. "I'll go along with your little charade, Amelia. So what do you expect us to do? I can only assume that you are looking for money for you and your baby and that you'll—"

"No! That's not it!" Amelia declared. "I don't want your money. When I get better, I plan to go back to work. I'm a licensed beautician in California. I will get a job in a beauty salon and—"

"And what about your child? If you're forced to support yourself, what happens to Jimmy while you're at work?"

"I'm not sure. I'll have to find someone to care for him and—"

"On a beautician's wages?" She frowned. "What kind of life do you think that would be for your child?"

Amelia knew exactly what kind of life it would be—and it was not what she wanted for Jimmy. She looked out the window to see that the sky had turned dark gray, almost the same color as Mrs. Bradley's fancy fur coat.

"What if we offered to keep Jimmy for you?" Mrs. Bradley's voice softened.

Of course, this proposition came as no surprise to Amelia . . . and yet the actual words jolted through her like an electrical shock. She turned to look at Mrs. Bradley, surprised to see an unexpected softness about her as she peered closely at Amelia. "Dr. Bradley and I are able to give Jimmy everything he needs in life—a comfortable home, two re-spectable parents, good education. What if Jimmy stayed here in Rockford with us, Amelia?" Her countenance grew warm. "I love little Jimmy," she said softly. "I would raise him as my own. As a result, he would have no social stigma attached to him—no one would know he was born out of wedlock. He might even grow up to be a fine doctor like my husband. I assure you that your boy would want for nothing if he remains with us."

Amelia's eyes were filling with tears, but she was deter-mined to hold them back.

"I know it will be a sacrifice," Mrs. Bradley said gently. "And I believe you did your best to care for him, Amelia. Despite his illness, which was quite serious, we could see that Jimmy was well cared for. He was clean and his clothing was of good quality."

"I—I made all of his clothes." Amelia fought back tears.

"A mother can make no finer sacrifice than to ensure her child a bright future. You have the power to do that, Amelia."

Amelia knew this was true. To hold on to Jimmy under these circumstances wasn't only selfish, it was irresponsible. As she locked eyes with Mrs. Bradley, she wondered what James would tell her to do. "You *really* do love him?" she questioned. "Would you love him like your own son? Or like the poor orphan you—"

"I promise you that I will raise him as my own son. Because I *do* love him, Amelia. I can't even explain it, and I suspect it has to do with losing my James and the emptiness I'd been feeling." She sighed. "For whatever reason, I felt an instant connection to little Jimmy. I believe I already do love him like my own son."

"And yet you refuse to believe he's James's son?"

Her expression cooled a bit. "As a child, I was taught to never speak ill of the dead, Amelia. I would ask you to do the same—at least where my James is concerned."

Amelia considered this. Perhaps it made no difference whether or not Mrs. Bradley believed Jimmy was James's son. The truth was the truth. And Mrs. Bradley was probably right—this might be the best way for Jimmy to grow up without the label of "illegitimate" always trailing him. That alone could ruin his life. Beyond all else, Amelia had to admit she had very little to offer her child. In fact, her poverty had nearly been the end of both of them. What right did she have to drag Jimmy back into deprivation? Especially when he could grow up like a prince with his paternal grandparents.

"I can see that you're considering my offer." Mrs. Bradley's expression grew warm again. "And I realize you might need time to think about it. This is a big decision. Not to be made lightly. I don't want to rush or push you. But my husband did mention that you are likely to be released from here by Friday."

"So I've heard." Part of Amelia wanted out of here, but another part was unsure . . . Where would she go? What would she do? What if she became sick again?

"So I will give you until Friday to make up your mind." Mrs. Bradley pulled on a pale gray glove as if getting ready to leave.

"I don't need that long." Amelia took in a slow, deep breath. "I know that Jimmy will be better off with you, Mrs. Bradley. And I—I do believe that you love him."

"I do! I really do."

"So I will agree—" Her voice cracked with emotion. "You can—can have him."

Mrs. Bradley reached for her hand, squeezing it. "I know this is hard on you, but I promise you, Amelia, you won't be sorry. Not for Jimmy's sake. I give you my word that your child will have a very fine life."

Amelia barely nodded, swallowing hard against the rock-hard lump growing in her throat.

"I'll have our attorney draw up legal papers and—"

"I—I have one request," Amelia said meekly.

"Yes?"

"I just want to see him once more . . . before I let him go. I want to say goodbye."

"Of course you do. As soon as you're released from here, we'll bring you to the house. You can see how well he's doing, and you can tell him goodbye." Mrs. Bradley had tears in her eyes too. Something Amelia found heartening. "I know this is painful, dear, but it really is for the best. You are giving your child a wonderful opportunity for an excellent life."

A tear trickled down Amelia's cheek. "I know," she admitted in a raspy voice. "Thank you, Mrs. Bradley."

She held up a finger. "I have one request too, Amelia. Please, call me Helene."

Amelia dipped her chin in an uneasy nod. "Okay. Helene."

"Naturally, we will cover all your travel expenses back to

California, as well as something to tide you over for about six months. That should give you time to find good employment. So you needn't worry about any of that." Helene stood, tugging on her other glove. "Just keep getting well, dear. I promised my husband I wouldn't stay too long . . . or upset you too much. Although he was well aware this would be an unsettling conversation for both of us."

Amelia just nodded. She knew that she'd made the best choice for Jimmy. But her heart felt as if a steamroller had just flattened it. And suddenly her own recovery felt irrelevant. She vaguely wondered if it was too late to have a complete relapse into pneumonia and perish. Or if it would even matter.

"You keep resting up, dear. And we will bring you to see Jimmy as soon as my husband says that you're well enough to be released."

Amelia mumbled a halfhearted thank-you, and Helene, apparently oblivious to her intense pain, picked up her lovely fur coat and handbag, gave a little wave with a gloved hand, and departed. As soon as she was gone, Amelia crumbled into full-blown sobs, followed by a fit of coughing. Certainly, she knew she'd done the right thing just now. The truth was she'd really made this decision that night when she'd deposited her beloved bundle in the manger. But the reality of it sliced through her like a knife.

14

On Friday morning, Amelia felt stronger, both physically and emotionally. She was resolved to do what was best for Jimmy. And she felt certain that James would have approved of her decision. His son would have the chance to grow up in a small town with a loving family. What more could she give?

It was nearly two when she was released from the hospital. The head nurse insisted on transporting her to the lobby in a wheelchair. "Dr. Bradley is just bringing the car around," she said as she parked Amelia in the vestibule by the front door. Dressed in her good blue suit, the same outfit she'd been wearing when Sally took her in . . . and later when she was transported to the hospital, she realized these garments had grown rather loose the past few weeks.

Amelia sighed as she gazed out the big picture window. The predicted snow had begun to fall the previous afternoon. Appreciative of the distraction, Amelia had watched in wonder as big white flakes had tumbled from the steely sky. It was the first time she'd ever seen real snow. And now the ground and trees and streetlamps were all blanketed in several inches of a fresh coat of clean white, sparkling so brightly against the clear blue sky that it made her eyes water.

To her relief, her misty eyes were not due to emotions . . . although the day was still young. Instead, the surprisingly pretty winter scene felt almost like medicine. Her spirits were elevated—if ever so slightly. The only problem was the cold vestibule. Every time someone went in or out, a swoosh of frosty air would chill her to the core. Even under the thick blanket that the nurse had insisted on wrapping around her, Amelia was shivering almost uncontrollably after a few minutes.

"There he is now." Nurse Gordon pointed to the sleek green Buick just pulling up. "Dr. Bradley's car is always so clean and pretty. Even after a blizzard."

The doctor waved as he got out and, hurrying over to open the passenger door, he quickly removed something bulky from inside. As he got closer to Amelia, she realized he had the same gray fur coat his wife had worn a few days ago. "Here." He slipped the heavy garment over her shoulders. "Helene was worried that you'd be cold."

"Oh, this is too fine—I can't possibly—"

"Helene insisted." He helped her to her feet. "And after all these years, I know better than to argue with my wife."

Soon she was loaded into the car, where the heater was running, and with the soft fur coat wrapped around her she soon began to feel warmer.

"I stopped by Sally's apartment like you asked," Dr. Bradley announced as he started to drive. "Your suitcase and things are in the trunk."

"Thank you."

"Sally sends you her best regards." He turned onto a tree-lined road. "I'm going to take the long way home. That will give us a chance to talk."

"Oh . . . okay."

"So . . . Helene has the paperwork ready. She's still over the moon that you've agreed to let us keep Jimmy." His voice sounded slightly stiff, as if he wasn't completely comfortable with their decision. "You're still sure about that?"

"Yes, that's right."

"I just need to know if she pressured you into this decision. Are you absolutely certain? I told her you were vulnerable, that she shouldn't push you. She didn't, did she?"

Amelia considered this. "No, no . . . not really. The truth is I think I had already made up my mind. That night when I placed Jimmy in your manger . . . in my heart I knew I was giving him up—for good."

"And is that because we are James's parents?"

"Yes, of course, that's a big part of it. He is, after all, James's child. Whether Mrs. Bradley accepts it or not, Jimmy *is* your grandson." She wanted to ask if Dr. Bradley believed her. She felt that he did, but they really hadn't spoken of it much.

"Well, as you know, Helene refuses to believe that James could have fathered a child. At least that's her claim. But I suspect that on some level she might be uncertain, and perhaps with time, as Jimmy grows up . . . well, I have a feeling she will eventually accept it. Especially if little Jimmy takes after James, like I'm guessing he will."

"I've decided that it's just as well if she doesn't accept Jimmy's true identity. It's a relief that Jimmy will grow up free from any stigma. I don't want his parents' mistakes to brand him for life. I feel confident that you and Mrs. Bradley can maintain his secret."

"Yes, we'll do what we can to protect him. After all, I've seen what happens in a small town . . . when rumors and innuendo float about and ruin a life." He glanced at her as he stopped for the traffic light on Main Street. "So how are you holding up, Amelia? I didn't get much of a chance to speak with you these last couple of days, but I know this must be very hard on you."

"Yes, but I realize it's best for Jimmy. There's no denying that." She took in a steadying breath. "And I hope that . . . in time . . . I will be better."

"Helene feels certain that you'll return to San Diego, is that right?"

She simply nodded, but the truth was she didn't have any real plans yet. Just say her goodbye to Jimmy . . . and make it through this day.

"I'm concerned about whether you're strong enough to make that long trip just yet. As your physician, I must insist you give yourself a few days to rest before you leave. I suggested you might stay in our home, but Helene felt that was unwise. She's worried that it might make it even harder for you to leave Jimmy."

Amelia thought about this, then nodded again. "I think she's right."

"For that reason, I've booked you a room at the Jackson."

"The Jackson?"

"That's our best hotel. I've booked the room for five days, but you're welcome to remain as long as you like. I really don't want you traveling until you're strong and fit." He pointed to a stately stone building. "There—that's the Jackson. And, believe me, it's a sight better than Wallace's."

As she thanked him, she ran a hand down the surface of the luxurious coat. She'd never felt fur this soft. "Is this coat real mink?"

He chuckled. "It is. And for Helene to insist on you wearing it is no small matter."

"It was very kind."

"Although Helene grew up in a very wealthy family, she isn't what I'd call a spendthrift. She is actually rather conservative about money. Her family, the Jacksons, founded this town—"

"Jackson? Same as the hotel?"

"Precisely. If you look around some, you'll see the Jackson name on a lot of things. They made their money copper mining."

"Oh."

"The reason I'm telling you this, Amelia, is because Helene plans to give you a check. She can afford to be generous. I hope that won't offend you."

"She mentioned that. And as much as I appreciate her help, it does make me a little uncomfortable," Amelia admitted.

"I wondered about that. But I hope you won't let it trouble you."

"I, uh, I don't want to feel like I'm, uh, selling my child."

"No one would ever believe that, Amelia. It's simply my wife's way of showing her appreciation." He pointed to the mink coat. "And the fact that she made me bring this for you tells me that she actually likes you, Amelia. Despite the circumstances that, well, make her uneasy, she does approve of you on many levels. And take it from me, Helene is a very discriminating woman."

"Really—she likes me?" Amelia felt a glimmer of hope. "That is encouraging."

"I'm aware that Helene has a reputation for being hard-nosed," he said. "But the truth is she has a very tender heart. She also has a very strong moral sense of right and wrong. Sometimes, at least in my opinion, it can be a bit too strong. But she is a good woman. Well respected in the community. And she's always been a fine mother."

"I believe that . . . just from knowing James."

Neither spoke for a long moment. Amelia remained transfixed on the snow-covered countryside all around her. The snow combined with the timbered landscape was truly breathtakingly beautiful. Jimmy would be happy here.

"How long did you know James?" Dr. Bradley asked gently.

"Not long enough." She sighed. "Oh, it felt longer at the time, but it really was a whirlwind romance. In just a few days, we both knew that we were in love. I was a bit surprised when James wanted to get married so quickly, but I gladly agreed. I knew he was the only one for me."

"The only one? Meaning you'll never marry again?"

She firmly shook her head no. "I can't imagine ever loving anyone the way I loved your son."

He made a sad smile. "This isn't something I can ever admit to Helene, but I can't help but derive some comfort knowing that you and James found each other . . . before . . . before he was taken from us. I've often said that God works in mysterious ways, Amelia, but I do believe this is one of those instances."

"I hope so . . . I mean, for Jimmy's sake."

"I imagine that someday, I'll better understand what God was up to down here. In the meantime, I just try to trust him."

"Yes, so do I." She knew they were close to the Bradleys' house now and suddenly she felt nervous. "As badly as I want to see Jimmy, I'm a bit afraid," she confessed as he turned down their street.

"Afraid? Of Helene?"

"No. Of myself. I don't want to break down and cry . . . Or what if I change my mind, and make a mess of everything?"

"It's your right to change your mind, Amelia. If you have any reservations about—"

"No," she said firmly. "I know it's for the best. I *know* it."

He slowed down to turn into their driveway, pointing at the nativity scene which, now blanketed in snow, had an even more ethereal sort of look. "Did you know that James built that?" He stopped the car so she could look at it better.

"No, I had no idea. But the first time I saw it, I was very impressed. It's beautiful. The faces look so lifelike. I assumed it was made by a professional."

"From an early age, James was a talented artist. Helene encouraged him to study architecture in college. But he gave up higher education after three and a half years. He'd spent his summers flying—ever since he was about sixteen. Helene hated it, but James was hooked. So just short of his degree, he quit college to help his brother-in-law, Harry, start a smoke jumper business."

"Yes, he told me about that. He flew the men in to jump into forest fires. It sounded very dangerous. But he just called it 'exciting.'"

"Their business was barely up and running when the war started, and much to Helene's chagrin, both James and Harry headed to San Diego to become Navy flyers."

"I know how much he loved flying." She stared in bittersweet wonder at the unique nativity scene. It was incredibly sad to think its creator was gone . . . but at least his son would be around to enjoy it. "I never realized James was such a gifted artist," she said quietly.

"James had so much potential. So much life to live." He sighed as he put the car back in gear. "Just one more reason we miss him so." He parked in front of the house. "Well, here we are. Home sweet home."

"There's something I'd like to get out of my suitcase, if you don't mind."

"Not at all." He helped her out of the car, going around to the back of the car.

As he opened the trunk, she explained about the marriage license James had filled out. "It's not that I'm trying to convince Mrs. Bradley of anything, but I'd like to leave it in your care—more for Jimmy's sake than anything. In case, well, in case anyone ever questions anything about his parentage." She opened her suitcase, then fished through it

MELODY CARLSON

until she found the big white envelope. "Here," she told him.
"Please, keep it in a safe place."

"Are you sure you don't want to hold onto it?"

She shook her head. "I want it available for Jimmy."

"Hello there." Helene waved from the front porch. "Come
in out of the cold, you two." A golden dog bounded toward
them, playfully running around Dr. Bradley as if to welcome
him home. It was sweet to think of Jimmy growing up in a
home with a big dog like this. She could imagine the little
boy tussling on the floor with the good-natured dog.

Amelia hurried up to greet Helene, thanking her for the
use of her wonderful coat. "It kept me warm as toast all the
way here." She carefully removed the garment as they came
into the foyer, handing it over to a housekeeper who was
standing by.

"Jimmy should be waking from his afternoon nap before
long, but you can go ahead and peek in on him in the nursery
if you like."

Amelia glanced around the elegant home. It was even nicer
on the inside than on the outside. Yet it wasn't opulent or
showy or overdone. In fact, despite its size, it had a nice,
homey feeling. With a fire crackling in the fireplace and comfortable furnishings and a rich-looking carpet, it was very
inviting. A wonderful place for a young child to grow up.
And the grounds outside were spacious and beautiful. She
looked out over the snow-covered side yard, trying to imagine
a preschool-aged Jimmy out there making a snowman with
Dr. Bradley. It was a touching picture.

She glanced over to where a baby bassinet trimmed in

blue was set up by an easy chair, reassured to see that Helene didn't keep Jimmy packed off in a room by himself all the time. "Where is the nursery?" Amelia asked her.

"Second floor." She pointed to an elegant wooden staircase. "It's the third door on your left. Nurse Doris is up there with him right now, but she knows you're coming."

Amelia thanked her, then headed slowly up the stairs. She could tell that her strength hadn't returned to her yet, and at the top landing, she felt surprisingly breathless. She paused to catch her breath, grateful that Helene hadn't insisted on accompanying her. She had probably known this was not going to be easy on Amelia.

Proceeding down the wide hallway, she came to the third door on the left to see that it was slightly ajar. She quietly pushed it open, staring at the sunny yellow bedroom. So cheerful and sweet. With a changing table, padded rocking chair, crib, and several other baby items, it made for a lovely nursery. Just the sort of nursery she had once dreamed of creating . . . when James returned and they found themselves a home.

A hard lump formed in her throat as she entered the nursery. A middle-aged woman with a kind face whispered a greeting, pointing to the crib before she quietly excused herself. With a pounding heart, Amelia approached the white crib. The last time she'd seen her child he'd been flushed and feverish, coughing and crying and frighteningly sick. But now he looked calm and at ease, sleeping peacefully with one tiny fist resting on his little chin. She leaned down to peer more closely at him. His blond curls were just as she remembered and he smelled so sweet that it brought tears to her eyes. He was obviously very well cared for. So much better than what she had to offer.

"I love you, my little darling." She leaned down to kiss a chubby cheek. "God bless you, my son." Her tears were coming fast now and she knew they'd be falling on Jimmy if she didn't finish this up. "I will always love you, James Junior . . . and I'll pray for you every day . . . but you will be better off here." She stood, using the back of her hands to wipe her wet cheeks. Then, without waking him, she turned and ran from the room and down the stairs to where the Bradleys were still standing in the front room.

"I'm ready to go," she announced in a thick, husky voice.

"That was so quick." Helene tilted her head to one side. "Are you sure?"

"I'm positive."

"Are you all right?" Dr. Bradley looked at her with concern. "Do you need a glass of water or anything?"

"No thank you. I just need to go." She was crying harder now.

"But the paperwork," Helene pointed to a desk where papers were laid out.

"Just show me where to sign." Amelia hurried over to the desk, grabbing up the fountain pen lying there.

"Maybe you should sit down." Dr. Bradley pulled out the chair, easing her into it. "Catch your breath and—"

"Just show me where to sign," she demanded again.

Helene came over, pointing out the lines awaiting Amelia's signature, watching and waiting until Amelia signed the last one and laid down the pen. "Jimmy is yours now." She looked directly at Helene as she stood. "I know you'll take excellent care of him. Th-thank you!" She hurried for the front door.

"Wait," Helene called out. "I have something for you."

Amelia stood by the door, waiting as Helene approached her with a long, thin envelope which obviously contained a check. "Thank you," Amelia managed to gasp. "I'm sorry I—I just can't contain my emotions. Forgive me."

"I'll take her to the hotel," Dr. Bradley told his wife.

"Wait," Helene said again.

Amelia didn't want to wait one more second, but she knew she had no choice. This time Helene had the mink coat over her arm. "Please, take this. I want you to have it, Amelia. I mean, to keep it."

Amelia's eyes grew wide. "But I can't—"

"Take it," Helene insisted with tears in her own eyes. "I will not let you say no to it. Take it! It will keep you warm while you're in town, and on your train trip." She thrust the coat into Amelia's arms, then turned and hurried away.

"But I can't accept—"

"Please, just take it!" Dr. Bradley opened the door. "It will be better for everyone if you do."

"But I—"

"Come on," he said brusquely, "let's get you to the hotel so you can rest. As your doctor, I'm concerned that you're barely out of the hospital and already you've overdone it. Doesn't reflect well on me." He hurried her into the car and now, with new snow starting to fall from the sky, he drove the few blocks to town. Neither of them said a word and soon he was parking in front of the fancy hotel.

Amelia's tears had slowed a bit by the time he helped her out of the car and into the lobby. To her relief, Dr. Bradley simply led her to a chair in the luxurious lobby. The chair was next to a tall Christmas tree. And to distract herself, she stared up at the glittering tree, but her tears made the colored lights blur together.

"Here you go." Dr. Bradley helped her to her feet, then handed her a brass key. "You're on the fifth floor and the elevator is over there." He opened his arms to embrace her, holding her tightly for several long seconds. "You're going to be okay."

"I know," she mumbled as he released her. "It's just hard—right now."

"You need to get some rest." He handed her a small brown bottle. "There are three tranquilizers in there. Take one when you get to your room. And another before bedtime—if you are still very upset and feel you need it. The last one is for tomorrow morning. But I suspect you won't need it by then."

"I'm sure I'll be fine by then." She forced a shaky smile.

"You know you can call me if you need anything, Amelia. Our phone number and other information is in the envelope Helene gave you. Along with a check."

"Thanks." She glanced at the bellboy coming toward them.

"And as your doctor, I must insist you stay indoors. Drink plenty of fluids, and order room service from the hotel's restaurant. Their food is quite good. I expect you'll be feeling like your old self in a few days."

She just nodded, mumbling another thank-you as the bellboy reached for her bag.

"Unless you are fit as a fiddle by next week—and I will be checking on you before then—I will insist you remain here longer." He tipped his hat, then left. The bellboy holding her suitcase grinned at her. "Right this way," he said politely, leading her to the elevator.

Before long he was setting her suitcase in what looked like a small, lovely living room. "Is there some mistake?" She frowned at the pretty space. There were even fresh flowers on the coffee table.

"This is our best suite." He pointed to a door to the right. "Bedroom over there. All the comforts of home." He grinned. "Just what the doctor ordered." He made a little salute. "And don't you worry, because the doctor already tipped me too."

<h1 style="text-align: center;">15</h1>

James's handmade calendar system had gotten left behind when the Japanese prison guards rushed to relocate him and the other prisoners about a week ago. Their new home, a little six-by-six insect-infested hut that he and his two buddies dubbed "the palace," was located deep in the interior of the small tropical island—the same island James and his two surviving crew members had been held captive on for most of this past year.

James's fighter plane had been shot down just south of the Philippine Islands last February. He and his navigator, Tony, and gunner, JT, had managed to stay afloat on a life raft for nearly a week after James's beloved Wildcat plunged into the Pacific. Sharing C-rations and what little liquid they could distill from seawater, their goal was to reach the safety of one of the Philippines' seven thousand islands.

Finally, severely dehydrated, sunburned, and starving, they spied an island. But just as they began paddling toward it, their lifeboat was spotted and captured by a Japanese

U-boat. The three were delivered to a Japanese prison camp on shore—and that was when the real suffering began.

As James lay on the thin grass mat that he'd carried from the previous prison camp, watching the first golden rays of sun shining between the cracks of the bamboo wall, his best guess was that it was mid December now—give or take. Not that it mattered. One day was pretty much the same as the next in a Japanese prison camp. Mostly James tried to avoid any unnecessary beatings by their ill-tempered guards, keep his eyes open for any possible food sources—including beetles and reptiles, and prevent JT and Tony from losing heart . . . or dying.

But lately there had been reason for hope. It started when their guards abruptly rounded up the dozen or so Allied inmates, marching them into the interior of the island. The rush suggested concerns about being discovered by liberating Allied forces, who would not be impressed by the way this POW camp had been managed. Their ruthless prison guards were either ignorant or ignoring the rules of the Geneva Conventions. As a result, a number of prisoners—weakened ones unable to make the trek—had been executed along the way. And if not for James and Tony, JT with his infected foot would've been among them.

Shortly after their arrival, they began to hear what sounded like US warplanes nearby. And random explosions to the south of them sounded like an invasion of sorts. At least that was their hope. But instead of reveling in this possibility, James was worried about a whole new threat—one he hadn't expressed to his buddies, but felt sure they suspected too.

The prison guards, fearful about a potential Allied invasion, might simply line up their detested prisoners, shoot them, and make a run for it. That was why, in this early hour, James had been trying to come up with some sort of escape plan. Not just for him and his buddies, but for all the prisoners. And that would not be easy.

He usually daydreamed about Amelia during this time of the morning. It was easier to imagine her beautiful face when all was calm and quiet and relatively cool in the POW camp. Before the day became unbearable. Because at the end of the day, when he was beaten—both physically and mentally—it was hard to think clearly about much of anything. So morning time was his Amelia time, and after asking for God's blessings on the upcoming day, he would treat himself with thoughts of Amelia.

He felt certain that daydreams about his fiancée had helped him to survive these long months of cruelty and deprivation. She had become his shining light and greatest motivation in surviving what felt like hell on earth. Sure, he loved his family and often thought of them, but it was memories of Amelia Richards that kept him going. She gave him the will to continue living—even at times when dying sounded like a relief.

"You asleep, Jim?" Tony's voice was hushed.

"Nah." James rolled over. Even beneath Tony's thin scruffy beard, James could see his friend's cheekbones. They were all severely malnourished.

"I feel like this is the end." Desperation filled his dark eyes. "Like we're gonna die in this godforsaken place. And no one will ever even know how it happened."

"Yeah . . . I was just thinking we need to get out of here."

"But how?"

"Did you hear how close those bombers got last night? Sounded like they were only about ten to fifteen miles away. It got me to thinking that we need to get to the coastline."

"How's that even possible?"

"We've got to overtake the guards."

"Yeah, but how?"

"I'm working on a plan. We'll take them out, and then we need to get down to the beach ASAP." James glanced over to where JT was still asleep.

"He'll never make it out on that foot," Tony whispered.

"I know." James frowned at JT's red, swollen limb. A centipede had bit him on the heel during the relocation, but now the infected area was turning black. Not a good sign.

"Even with the crutch you made him, he's not going to get far."

James nodded glumly. These were all things he'd already considered.

"What if we leave him here?" Tony whispered. "You and me make a break for it in the middle of the night—we go as fast as we can for the coastline. Then we find help and come back for him and the others?"

"It won't work," James told him. "If we leave, the guards will take it out on the other prisoners. We need to get everyone out of here. Anyone left behind won't have a chance."

"How?" Tony frowned. "What's your plan?"

"Remember the machetes we were allowed to use—to build our huts?"

148

"Yeah, but they're locked up in that chest."

James pointed to JT. "Remember what he told us about the jewel thief uncle that taught him to pick a lock?"

"Yeah, but that was just big talk."

"Maybe not." James gently poked JT in the shoulder, giving him a moment to wake up. "How you doing, buddy? That foot doesn't look too good."

JT sat up with a painful groan.

"We gotta get outta here," Tony told JT. "Jim's got a plan."

"It'll probably sound crazy, but it might be our only chance." James explained what he'd been thinking, about how they could get some of the prisoners to create a smoke screen on the opposite side of the camp. "We'll do it while we're on forage patrol. The distraction needs to be big enough to get the attention of all three guards, but not dangerous enough to get anyone shot. JT, while the guards are preoccupied, we'll get you to the storage trunk and you can pick the lock. We'll grab the machetes and hide them in the brush. Then, later on when the guards are having their midday meal, we'll sneak in several of the strongest men and, armed with machetes, we'll ambush the guards." He grimaced. "I know it's a long shot, but we need to take it."

"You mean kill them before they kill us?" JT said in a flat tone.

"You know how it works . . . If they think the Allies are coming, it's in their best interest to get rid of us."

"'Cuz dead men don't talk," Tony said solemnly. "Neither will the guards when we're through with 'em."

"Maybe . . . But if we jump them fast enough, we might not even have to kill them. We'll just tie them up good and tight and leave them here for the insects to finish off."

JT almost smiled. "Yeah, I'd like to see that."

A few hours later, after sharing their strategy amongst the other prisoners, James led the men in his plan. The smoke screen involved several men claiming to have found a wild boar while foraging for food—and then a "fight" ensued over who would keep the prize. Since the guards' food supplies, though highly superior to the prisoners, were still limited, their interest in confiscating fresh pork was high.

In the meantime, James and Tony transported JT to the storage chest where, armed with several stick tools he'd made earlier, he cleverly managed to pick the lock. James and JT had just removed the machetes and thrown them into the nearby bush by the time the guards discovered there was no pig. The prisoners acted as if the boar had gotten away, which simply aggravated the guards, resulting in a loud scolding and some hard whacks with their rifle butts. But by now the storage chest was closed, James and Tony had helped JT get back to their forage patrolling, and the guards were none the wiser.

As usual, they sat down to eat in the heat of the day—the time when no one had much energy—and that's when five men, led by James, crawled through the brush to get the machetes. After dividing into two groups, they snuck all the way around the camp into position. James imitated a bird call as a signal, and they all leaped into action.

The three guards were caught so completely off guard that the machete-armed prisoners were able to easily secure their firearms.

"Let's kill them and get it over with," a prisoner named Ralph shouted.

"Yeah, they deserve to die," another agreed.

"No," James reminded them in a tough tone. "We agreed to tie them up if we got their guns without a fight, and that's just what we're going to do." He yelled out to the other prisoners, commanding everyone to help out with the various tasks until the three guards were bound and gagged.

"And now it's time for lunch," Tony held up a partially eaten bowl of rice.

"Let's divide up their food," James instructed the others. "Everyone, have some nourishment now, and we'll take the rest of their food for our trek to the coastline. We need to move fast."

They took turns helping to carry JT on a travois that James and Tony quickly constructed from bamboo and rope, slowly making their way through the jungle toward the coastline. They knew they weren't too far off when they made camp for the night, and started out at daybreak, arriving at the beach by midday. They could still hear planes flying nearby and occasional bombs being dropped. After using coconuts and vegetation to write a giant message on the beach—POW ALLIES HERE—they waited anxiously, dining on fish and coconuts and rice, until they were eventually spotted by a Navy plane that circled about as they danced around on the beach. The plane dipped its wings to signify that they'd been observed. The following morning, they were rescued by a landing craft, which transported them to an aircraft carrier where they received preliminary medical treatment and food.

"JT lost his foot," Tony informed James on their second day. Severely dehydrated, James was still in the infirmary, but Tony must've been built of sturdier stuff because he was out and about and doing as he pleased.

"Tell JT I'm sorry," James said solemnly. "Is he going to be okay? I mean, besides the amputation. He was in pretty bad shape when they picked us up."

"Removing that foot probably saved his life." Tony lit up a cigarette. "And he has you to thank for making it out alive. We all do."

"We all did it . . . *together.*"

"Anyway, JT can't be transported for a week or so, but it sounds like the rest of us will be stateside soon." He grinned. "Can you believe it? We'll be home for Christmas!" And now Tony was doing a little jig around the infirmary. It was hard to believe this was the same guy who'd felt like giving up just days ago.

James, like some of the other surviving prisoners, wasn't quite as resilient as Tony. Being treated for malnutrition and several parasitical diseases, he wasn't ready to jump up and dance quite yet. And it was still hard to grasp that they had really made it out alive. Just thinking about their ordeal was so overwhelming that it was difficult to put into words when he was interviewed by the ship's psychologist. But the thought of being in the USA soon—and seeing Amelia again—did make him want to dance!

16

It was less than a week before Christmas when James and the other prisoners landed in Honolulu. The plan was to keep them there a day or two—just until a flight to the mainland could be arranged. The men were taken directly to the hospital, where they received more medical exams and care, as well as good food. By now James was able to keep down more than just clear soup, but due to his low weight and general health, he was still confined to the hospital bed. At least the place was bright and cheery. The nurses had decorated it for Christmas, even bringing in a palm tree that they'd strung with lights. So the general atmosphere was surprisingly lighthearted and jovial. Especially considering the serious condition of some of the less fortunate patients. James realized that, despite his year of hardship, he had much to be thankful for.

"I'd like to send a couple of telegrams," he told the nurse who had just checked his vital signs, "to let my loved ones know that I'm okay."

"Do you want me to take care of that for you?" She looked up from her clipboard.

"I know you're pretty busy, but I would appreciate it." Not wanting to waste too much of her time, James quickly dictated a short note to his parents, notifying them that he was alive and well, and that he would call them as soon as he was stateside. "And now for my fiancée . . ." He wanted to come up with just the right words, then decided to keep it short and simple. "Dear Amelia—stop. I'm coming home—stop. Will see you in a few days—stop. Let's get married ASAP—stop. Love James—stop."

"I won't be able to get these out until after my shift ends. Is that okay?"

"Sure, that'll be fine." He gave her his parents' address in Rockford and the name of the women's hotel where Amelia had been living before he left last January. It was hard to believe that he'd met her less than a year ago . . . it felt like a lifetime. But it would all be worthwhile when he could hold her in his arms again.

To James's surprise, he was released from the hospital just a few hours later. More beds were needed because of a rash of incoming patients. He felt sorry for the nurses, scurrying about and getting everything ready. But he felt even more sorry when he saw the severely wounded sailors being wheeled in. All were in much worse shape than him—a grim reminder that this war was far from over.

Just the same, he was relieved to be out of the confines of the hospital. And despite his promise to the doctor—to continue a healthful diet and take it easy—James was enjoying his newfound freedom wandering about Honolulu with Tony.

It wasn't until they were on the flight to San Diego that Tony questioned something. "Do you think our telegrams really got sent home?"

"What do you mean?"

"I just got to thinking how crazy everything was in the hospital—remember right before we were released the other day? I wouldn't be surprised if that nurse forgot all about sending our telegrams." He grinned. "I kinda hope she didn't send them."

"Why?"

"I like the idea of surprising my family. Think about it. I walk into the house at Christmastime and they all fall out of their chairs from the shock of it." He laughed loudly. "I can just imagine Great-Aunt Gladys fainting in her eggnog."

James considered this. Maybe it would be fun to catch his loved ones off guard like that. In fact, it might be fortunate if his parents hadn't received his telegram yet. That way he wouldn't feel guilty for spending more time with Amelia in San Diego. Although he just really wanted to sweep his sweetheart off her feet and take her home with him. Now that would make for a perfect Christmas!

By the time James was walking around in San Diego, it was just a few days before Christmas. He was still extremely underweight and wearing a uniform many sizes smaller than normal, but he felt strong and good—and all he wanted was to reunite with Amelia. Since it was a weekday morning, his plan was to surprise her at the beauty parlor where she worked—and then he would whoosh her away with him to Montana. He would introduce her to his family . . . and make her his wife! Maybe they could have a New Year's Eve wedding—a way to commemorate the night they first met one whole year ago.

He took in a deep breath, removed his hat, and entered the beauty parlor where Amelia worked. Everything looked the same—shiny and pink. It even smelled the same—a weird mix of perfume and chemicals. He wondered how Amelia could stand it day after day. Well, hopefully, she wouldn't have to. Not after today! He smiled at the receptionist and tried to hide his impatience.

"Amelia Richards? She left us quite some time ago," the receptionist informed him. "I think it was March—or April. But it's been a while."

"Oh?" He frowned. "Do you know where she works now?"

She just shook her head. Feeling slightly discouraged, James decided to make an inquiry at the women's hotel. Surely they would know where she worked. But when he got to the hotel, which was only a few blocks away, he was told that she had moved from there—last spring.

"Did a telegram arrive here for her?" he asked with mild curiosity.

"No. We haven't received any telegrams lately."

He considered this. It had been almost two days since the telegram was wired from Honolulu. "You're sure? It should've arrived by yesterday at the latest. Maybe it was returned because Amelia wasn't here."

"No telegrams have been delivered," she firmly told him.

James thanked her, then went to use the pay phone in the hotel's lobby. His plan was to call every beauty parlor listed in the phone book if necessary. Starting with AAA Beauty Shop, he was determined not to give up until he called Zelda's Hair Salon—or located Amelia. To his relief, he hit pay dirt when the receptionist at Alliette's Beauty Parlor confirmed that Amelia had recently worked there. "She only quit a few weeks ago," the woman told him. "She left right before Thanksgiving."

"Do you know where I can reach her? Where she's working?" he asked.

"I'm sorry, I don't. I do know she moved from San Diego, but I'm not sure where. Although Claudine could probably help you. She's a hairdresser here, and they were roommates."

"May I speak to Claudine?"

"Sorry. She's gone to visit her family in Texas and won't be back until after Christmas."

"Is there anyone else there who might know Amelia's whereabouts?"

"Not that I know of."

He wanted to question her further, but she cut the conversation short, saying she had a customer to attend to. "Merry Christmas," she said cheerfully, then hung up.

"Merry Christmas," he repeated glumly as he replaced the receiver. What to do now? He considered calling his parents to let them know he would soon be home, but he felt so discouraged about not finding Amelia that he didn't want to speak to anyone. Perhaps it would be better to simply surprise them. He knew he could catch a ride in a cargo plane going from San Diego to Seattle later this afternoon. From there the train trip was only seven or eight hours. If he took a late evening train, he would arrive by morning—and hopefully be in better spirits to greet his family. Somehow he would get through the holidays. And then he would return to San Diego and hire a private detective to locate Amelia.

But later, as he rode in the noisy cargo plane, sitting in the back amidst the boxes of supplies, he started to think . . . What if Amelia had gotten married to someone else? What if she'd given up on him, been swept up by another man? She was so sweet and smart and beautiful . . . What man wouldn't want her for his wife?

By the time he got on the late-night train, he felt thoroughly discouraged—and exhausted. But at least he was going home, where he imagined he might sleep for a week. At least he'd be well cared for there. Between his overly protective mother and Doctor Dad, he would be in good hands. And their attentions would actually be welcomed for a change. As the porter set his bag in the sleeping car, James tipped him and asked for a wake-up call before Rockford. Then, feeling even more hopeless than he'd been during his imprisonment, James went to bed.

Amelia had never in all her life been treated so well. Staying in the presidential suite, which the bellhop informed her had never hosted a real president, she felt like royalty. And with the hotel's festive Christmas decorations and holiday cookies served by the fireplace every afternoon—not to mention the excellent food and room service—it was like being a guest at a long, lovely holiday party. So much so that it was difficult to check out of the Jackson Hotel. It had almost started to feel like home. A very luxurious home. The only thing missing was Jimmy. But she'd been trying not to think about that. She wasn't sure she'd ever be able to think about her baby without breaking into tears.

"I hope you enjoyed your stay with us," the desk clerk politely said as she checked out in the early morning.

"Very much so."

"Going home for the holidays?" He gave her a receipt.

She wasn't sure how to answer that, but returning his smile, she simply nodded. The truth was she had no home. Perhaps she never would. Maybe it no longer mattered. What use was a home if you had no family? Even when she'd tried to call Claudine, hoping she might be able to stay with her a bit, no one had answered. Not in the morning and not even at night. And so Amelia planned to just stay in a hotel during the holidays. Or maybe she'd return to the women's hotel where she'd lived before . . . if they had an available room.

"Looks like your ride is here." The clerk nodded toward the front door.

She turned to see Dr. Bradley just coming in. She'd told him it wasn't necessary for him to take her to the train station this morning, but he had insisted—not only on taking her but also on purchasing her ticket.

"Good morning." He smiled as she returned his greeting, but his eyes were sad. "Let me take that." He reached for her bag. "How are you doing?"

"I'm fine," she said in a tight voice.

"Ready for the long train trip?"

She just nodded, pulling the mink coat more snugly around her as they stepped outside to where snow was blowing in circles.

He hurried to the car, opening the passenger door for her. After they were both in the car, she tried to think of something to say. She wanted to ask how Jimmy was doing, but she knew what the answer would be. Jimmy was better than ever, putting on more weight, probably smiling—and who knew what else. She really didn't want to know, didn't want to break into uncontrollable tears.

Instead, she thanked Dr. Bradley for her time at the hotel. "I felt like a princess. So luxurious. And my suite was so beautiful, with a view looking out over the town all blanketed in snow. The scene reminded me of a Currier and Ives Christmas card. The hotel staff was so nice. And the decorations were so pretty." She knew she was rambling, but she simply wanted to fill the empty space between them.

"Well, I'm glad you got rested up." He glanced at her as he stopped at the traffic light. "Good to see you have some color back in your cheeks."

"It looked like some guests planned to spend the holidays at the hotel," she continued absently. "I got to see some happy reunions in the lobby." She didn't mention that witnessing the serviceman being greeted by his wife and children had made her unbearably sad . . . and lonely. That would only make everything worse. "I hope that you and your family have a good Christmas." She forced a smile as he pulled in front of the train station.

"Thank you." He got out and, after getting her suitcase, helped her out of the car.

"You don't need to go inside." She reached for her suitcase. "Thank you for all your help, Dr. Bradley." That familiar lump had returned to her throat. "I know you will take excellent care of Jimmy and—" Her voice cracked with emotion as he wrapped his arms around her in a goodbye hug.

"You'll be okay, Amelia." He patted her back and stepped away. "You are a very resilient young woman. I know you will find your way. Just give yourself time."

She nodded, still holding back tears.

"Be sure and write to us when you get settled. Give us your address and we'll send photos of Jimmy like I promised."

She thanked him again, then saying a hasty goodbye she turned and hurried into the station. The train wasn't due for about twenty minutes, enough time for her to get a cup of coffee and hopefully pull her emotions under control. It still felt strange to be wearing Mrs. Bradley's mink coat, but she had to admit it was cozy, and it was amusing to see people treating her with more respect. Just for a coat?

Finished with her coffee, she went over to the waiting area, watching as the train slowly pulled into the station. She picked up her suitcase and slowly made her way to the platform, watching as passengers disembarked from the train. She felt a catch in her chest as she watched a tall, thin man stepping off of the train. She knew it was the Naval officer's uniform that had caught her eye. So common in San Diego, but not so much here in Rockford. But as the man walked toward the station, she blinked in disbelief and then did a double take.

"James?" She gasped, feeling so light-headed that it seemed the whole platform and everyone on it was spinning—like a kaleidoscope of color and sound and motion.

"*Amelia!*" He dropped his duffle bag and raced toward her, swooping her into his arms just as her knees gave way.

When she returned to her senses, she was sitting on a bench with James's arm wrapped snugly around her and a strange woman offering her a paper cup of water. She held up her hand to reject the water then turned to stare into James's face. "It really is you," she whispered. "I can't believe it."

"It's true, darling." He leaned toward her, landing a reassuring kiss on her lips. "And it's really you."

She reached up to touch his face. Although his skin was tanned, he was too thin and looked aged. "You're not dead."

He smiled and his blue eyes lit up with the warmth she remembered. "I'm very much alive." Holding her hand, he told her about his plane being shot down and being captured by the Japanese. "My crew and I were held on an island in the Philippines until just a few days ago. I tried to send you a telegram from Honolulu, but—"

"Your parents!" she said suddenly. "They don't know either, do they?"

"I tried to send them a telegram too." He frowned. "But maybe they didn't get it yet. It got awfully busy at the hospital right before I shipped out."

"Oh, James. I have so much to tell you." She looked around the train station, relieved to see that the small crowd of curious onlookers had moved on. "But not here."

"What are you doing in Rockford?" he asked as they gathered their bags.

"It's a long story." She clutched his elbow with her free hand, determined not to let go—ever! Then hoping this wasn't all just a dream—if it was a dream, she hoped to never wake up!—she tried to walk steadily through the train station.

"Where should we go to talk?" he asked as they went outside. The snow was falling harder now, and she could see that he was shivering.

"To your house," she declared. "Your parents need to know you're alive, James. The sooner the better!"

He waved for a taxi, and it wasn't long until they were driving into the Bradley driveway and past the snow-covered nativity scene. "Hey, they still use that old thing." James laughed.

"It's a beautiful old thing," she told him. "I love it." To her relief, Dr. Bradley's car was parked in front. It was probably too early for him to go to his clinic. "Your parents are in for such a shock," she said nervously. She glanced at James as he pressed the doorbell. "And so are you, darling. So are you . . ."

CHRISTMAS DAY, 1944

The Christmas wedding held in the Bradley home was small and private and intimate. And in Amelia's opinion, everything—from the twelve-foot-tall Christmas tree to the numerous shimmering candles illuminating the front room— was absolutely perfect. She couldn't have dreamed of a more beautiful ceremony.

James's darling sister Grace loaned Amelia her own wedding dress—a beautiful gown of ivory satin that, although a bit long, fit remarkably well otherwise. Grace, wearing a dark green velvet gown, stood up as Amelia's matron of honor. James's brother-in-law and best friend, Harry, performed the services of best man wearing his Navy officer's dress uniform that was identical to James's. Their sweet daughter, Janie, dressed in a red velvet dress and carrying a bouquet of pink poinsettias, was the flower girl. Little Jimmy, happily nestled in his daddy's arms, was dressed in a white suit complete with a tiny pocket that contained two bands of gold.

Helene and George wore their finest—along with happy faces. Goldie, who wore a big red bow, and the household staff were the only other wedding guests in attendance. That suited the wedding couple just fine. The Bradleys' old family friend, the respectable Reverend Thompson, officiated the double-ring ceremony—and his words were both eloquent and gracious.

But it was James's beaming face—as Amelia came down the poinsettia-lined staircase—that would remain fixed in her mind forever. He looked just as happy as she felt. And seeing him waiting for her, surrounded by his loving family, holding his infant son in his arms—well, it was absolutely perfect.

The wedding couple enjoyed a lovely wedding feast of roast beef and all the trimmings. As they all sat around the big table, Amelia knew she'd never felt so much at home or part of a family than she did right now. After Amelia and James put Jimmy to bed, Amelia changed out of her wedding clothes. She was just buttoning the jacket of her good blue suit when she heard a gentle tapping on the door.

"Mrs. Bradley." Amelia smiled, opening the door wider.

"Helene," she reminded her as she came in.

"Yes, I'm sorry. Helene." Amelia nodded.

"This is for you." Helene held up a pretty corsage of delicate white flowers. "For your honeymoon." She carefully pinned it to Amelia's lapel then stepped back to look at her. "I know I've already apologized to you . . . for not believing you, but—"

"You know that all is forgiven," Amelia told her. "And I'm so grateful you forgave me too."

Helene waved her hand. "Of course. But I just wanted to tell you something else, Amelia. I am proud to call you my daughter-in-law. James picked a lovely woman to become his bride . . . and the mother of his son. I approve."

Amelia blinked back tears of joy, throwing her arms around Helene. "Thank you—that means so much to me." After she stepped back from the spontaneous embrace, she waved to where Helene's coat was neatly laid out on the spare room bed. "I meant to give that back to you earlier, but it's been so busy—"

"No, that's yours now." Helene went over to pick up the coat.

"But it's too—"

"I insist, Amelia. I want you to keep it. And whenever

you wear it just remember it's like your mother-in-law giving you a hug." She smiled as she slipped it over Amelia's shoulders.

"Thank you so—"

"The bridegroom cometh," James announced. "Is the bride ready?"

"Yes, she is," Helene called back to him.

As they went down the stairs, they were greeted by their wedding guests and a few handfuls of rice. With his arm around her, James escorted her past them and out to where his car was waiting—appropriately decorated with streamers and even some old shoes tied to the bumper.

"This has been the best Christmas of my life," James declared as he helped her into the passenger seat. "You and Jimmy have made me the happiest man on earth."

"I never dreamed I could be this happy," she said as he leaned in to kiss her. "Not in a million years."

He drove slowly down the driveway, stopping by the nativity scene that was glimmering in the snow and spotlights. He chuckled quietly as he slowly shook his head. "I still can't believe you put Jimmy in my manger." He grinned and reached for her hand, giving it a warm squeeze. "But I'm so glad you did."

"I was so desperate . . . so lost," she said quietly.

"Well, now you are found, Mrs. Bradley." Then he drove them to the Jackson Hotel, where—to her surprised delight—he had managed to reserve the presidential suite for their honeymoon. Amelia couldn't help but giggle as he carried her across the threshold.

"You're supposed to carry your bride like that when you enter your own home," she teased, "not a hotel."

"You *are* home," he said solemnly. "When you're with me, Amelia, you are home. Both you and Jimmy. Welcome home, darling!" And he sealed it with a kiss.

Melody Carlson is the award-winning author of over two hundred books, including *Christmas at Harrington's*, *The Christmas Pony*, *A Simple Christmas Wish*, *The Christmas Cat*, and *The Christmas Joy Ride*. Melody has received a *Romantic Times* Career Achievement Award in the inspirational market for her books. She and her husband live in central Oregon. For more information about Melody, visit her website at www.melodycarlson.com.

Meet Melody at
MelodyCarlson.com

- Enter a contest for a signed book
- Read her monthly newsletter
- Find a special page for book clubs
- Discover more books by Melody

Become a fan on Facebook
Melody Carlson Books

"A summer of new beginnings becomes a summer of unexpected love."

—**Lisa Wingate**, bestselling author of *The Prayer Box* and *The Story Keeper*

Anna moved to New York City looking for her big break and hoping for love—she just didn't imagine both would depend on a familiar face.

Revell
a division of Baker Publishing Group
www.RevellBooks.com

Available wherever books and ebooks are sold.

She's anticipating a quiet summer surrounded by beauty. She never expected a fresh chance at love.

When an art teacher moves to Savannah to manage an art gallery for the summer, she finds far more than she anticipated as two handsome brothers vie for her attention.

Revell
a division of Baker Publishing Group
www.RevellBooks.com

Available wherever books and ebooks are sold.

Printed in the United States
By Bookmasters